fantasies of the body

Also by David Plante

The Ghost of Henry James (1970)
Slides (1971)
Relatives (1972)
The Darkness of the Body (1974)
Figures in Bright Air (1976)
The Family (1978)
The Country (1980)
The Woods (1982)
Difficult Women (1983)
The Foreigner (1984)
The Catholic (1986)
My Mother's Pearl Necklace (1987)
The Native (1987)
The Accident (1991)
Annunciation (1994)
Prayer (1998)
The Age of Terror (1999)
American Ghosts (2005)
ABC (2007)
The Pure Lover (2009)
Becoming a Londoner: A Diary (2013)
Worlds Apart: A Memoir (2015)
American Stranger (2018)
Eternity (2024)

Fantasies of the Body

a novel

DAVID PLANTE

GREEN CITY BOOKS
Bend, OR

ISBN: 9781963101126
First Edition
designed by Isaac Peterson
cover design by Isaac Peterson
Library of Congress Cataloging-in-Publication Data has been applied for.

23 24 LSC 10 9 8 7 6 5 4 3 2 1

From E.M. Forster's *The Longest Journey*:

Cambridge had taken him and soothed him, and warmed him, and had laughed at him a little, saying that he must not be so tragic yet awhile.

Stewart Ansell asked his father, "At Cambridge, can I read for the Moral Science Tripos?"

Mr. Ansell had only replied, "This philosophy—do you say that it lies behind everything?"

"Yes, I think so. It tries to discover what is true and good."

"Then, my boy, you had better read as much of it as you can."

He looked at the face, which was frank, proud, and beautiful, if truth is beauty. A silence, akin to poetry, invaded Ansell.

Ansell said, with irritation, "But what can you expect from a person who's eternally beautiful?"

Rickie thought, Do such things actually happen? Was Love a column of fire? Was he a torrent of song?

When Rickie said that nothing beautiful was ever to be regretted, "You're cracked on beauty," she whispered—they were still inside the church. "Do hurry up and write something."

"Something beautiful?"

"I believe you can. Take care that you don't waste your life."

He revisited Cambridge, and his name was a gray ghost over the door.

"I have been too far back," said Rickie gently. "Ansell took me on a journey that was even new to him. We got behind right and wrong, to a place where only one thing matters—that the Beloved should rise from the dead."

Let us love one another. Let our children, physical and spiritual, love one another. It is all that we can do.

One.

A friend asked me to stay in his apartment across the Charles River in Cambridge to take care of his cat while he was away, and, thinking I was about to give up my small room for another larger one, I accepted.

With the cat, I sat in an armchair and read from the many books in the apartment.

Every day, I went by train over the Charles River to teach at the language school.

I had a few friends, and at a party in the house of a male couple, I met someone named William. As we were walking together to the subway station nearby, he said he could spend the night at the Spee Club at Harvard, but since this was a holiday, he would find that the linens had been locked away.

I didn't want to ask him what the Spee Club was, but I knew that it was a club for Yankees.

He was tall. His hair, cut short above his ears and at his nape and a little wavy on top, was blond-brown, and his eyes were blue. He wore a blazer and a thin tie, the collar of his shirt stiff and sharp-edged.

He was beautiful.

If he couldn't stay at his club, I said, he could stay with me.

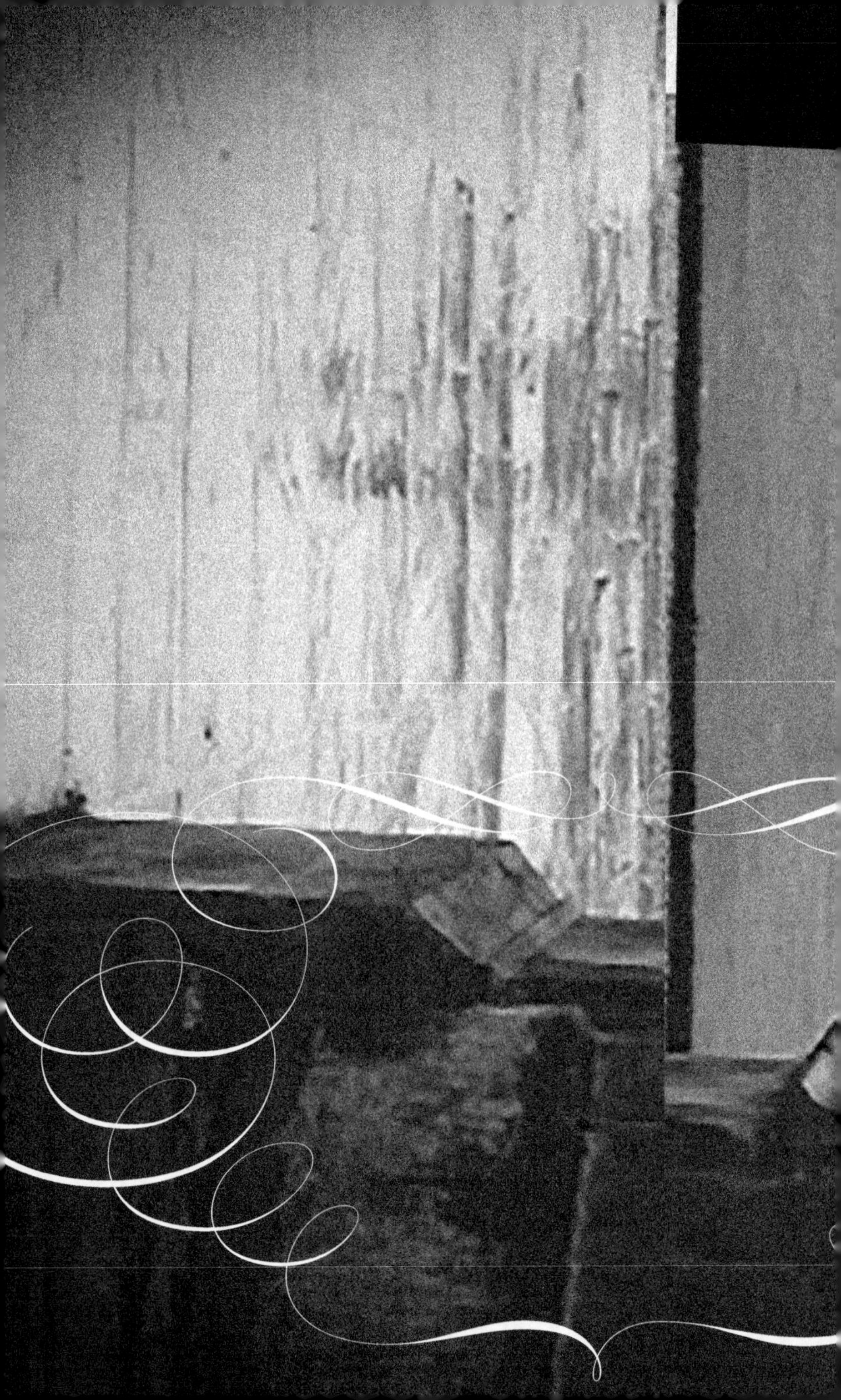

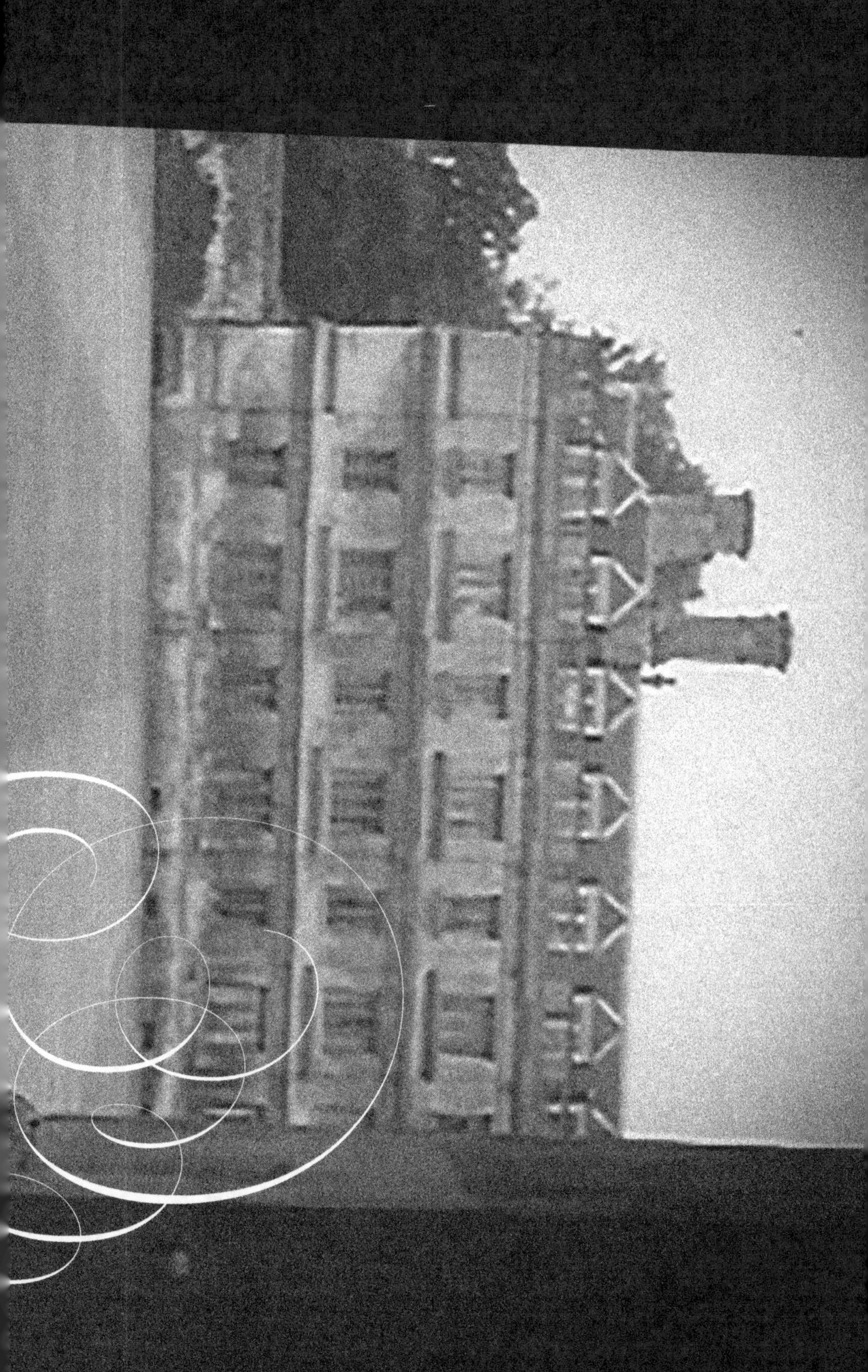

The dark November sky was clear. We walked together to my apartment.

I told him he could either sleep on the couch in the living room or with me.

He would sleep with me.

I hadn't made love in months, and I shouted so that William put a hand over my mouth.

The reserved Yankee I had met now naked, lay beside me in my bed. Nothing, I thought, nothing is more beautiful than that: the body of another.

After William left, I remained for a while with the effects of our love-making all over me, a thick skin of dry sperm and saliva and sweat.

Wandering about the living room, I took a book down from a shelf and opened it and read:

Your face possesses my despair

This was a line of poetry, and it centered all my attention, and at the center appeared a circle of dark, and at the center the face.

I read:

How much it aches to linger in these things!
I thought the perfect end of love was peace
After the long-forgiven suffering.
But something else, I know not what it is,

The words that come so near and then not,
The vanity, the error of the whole,
The strong cross-purposes, oh, I know not what

Cries dreadfully in the distracted soul—

The poet was Trumbull Stickney; he lived from 1874 to 1904, only thirty years, and he was, I saw from the photograph of his in the book, beautiful.

A contemporary of his at Harvard had said he was "brilliant," had "a figure supple and graceful as a Greek runner's." But he was not accepted because, for example, in commenting on a sunset, he used the word *gorgeous*. I tried to imagine the poet, taller than the others, pointing over their heads, his face bright in the sunlight, and saying it was "gorgeous," and humiliating himself.

William hadn't left me with any way of getting in touch with him, and before he'd left, he hadn't taken my telephone number, so I assumed he didn't want to see me again. I was sorry for this, but, however much I had made love with others, I had learned not to force myself on anyone, as I had been accused of doing. But I did yearn for him, and though I could have eased this yearning by going out to a bar and picking up someone, I held back.

A few days later, on my return from teaching, in coarse, cold, autumn mist, I saw William in a long overcoat, standing among fallen leaves under the maple tree outside the brick apartment building where I lived.

He said, quietly, that he had suspected I would be arriving back at this time.

Inside, in the warmth, his blond face shone in the cold. I grabbed him even before he was able to take off his gloves.

I expected William to spend the night. In bed with me, he said it must be nice to be settled in an apartment of one's own.

I told him I was there only until my friend returned. I asked if he had a place of his own.

He told me that just before he met me, he had returned from London, where he had lived for three years. He had been at King's College Cambridge, where he had read, he said, Classics, meaning Latin and Greek. He preferred Greek to Latin.

Why had he left London to return to Boston?

He said he had to.

I understood from his references to Louisburg Square, Prides Crossing, Ipswich, to aunts in big houses with whom he had tea, that William belonged to a large and complex old Yankee family demanding in its expectations; now that he was in Boston, he had to do more than teach fencing at Harvard, had to enter a proper firm, and hadn't he any intention of marrying?

In his absence in the morning, I found a note:

Please keep my visits to you a secret.

This suggested there would be more visits. I wasn't sure I wanted to see him again, for if I had been warned not to impose myself on another, I didn't want anyone to impose himself on me. And yet, I did want to see him, but, again, had no way of communicating with him, nor did he have a way of communicating with me.

Only a week remained before my friend returned. I put a deposit on another, larger room, on Beacon Hill. Back at the apartment in Cambridge, I again found William outside, standing under the maple tree that had now lost its leaves. He said hello, as if he had no reason to say anything more. I didn't expect him to say more.

We ate a cold supper, during which William talked about ancient Greek epigrams. He recited one in Greek, and I asked him to translate: "His bones gleamed naked on a foreign shore."

I went ahead of him into the bedroom and undressed and got into bed. He came in and I watched him undress.

Next to me in bed, he said he was very tired.

I said we'd sleep.

I woke when his body jerked and I put my arms about him and kissed his forehead, and I fell back to sleep.

We woke during the early morning, he perhaps still half asleep and I did not quite know who I was any more than I knew he was. And we made love.

He all at once wrenched away from me and got out of bed. I heard him dress and—I had no idea at what time in the dark morning—leave.

I left the apartment the day my friend returned and moved to my room on Beacon Hill. I went to the school for my day's teaching. It was raining when I left the school. Walking to my room in the rain, I realized I hadn't told William where I'd be.

This came to me: I needed him. I needed to make love with him.

From a booth in the street, I telephoned the friend whose apartment I had been staying in to tell him that if someone named William stopped by to tell him, please, where I now was.

The rain had stopped, the sun had come out. I walked through the Boston Common. There was no one else along the path. The red light of the sun shone on the bare, black, wet branches of the trees, and in the sunlight, I saw, as if what I saw inwardly was reversed by a sudden optical spasm, the naked body of William. I had to stop myself from kneeling and pressing my forehead to the ground, weak with my love for that beautiful body.

I arrived in my room just as the telephone was ringing. My mother wanted to let me know that an uncle had died. As I had the next day off from teaching, I went by train to Providence and took a bus to the parish for the funeral.

The body of my uncle in his casket, the skin of his face smoothed to his skull, was surrounded by flowers. I had never seen him wear a tie, not even at church; he had always worn a checked flannel shirt, the collar buttoned tightly about his wrinkled neck. His Christian name was Napoleon. My aunt, who had a large mole on her forehead, hugged me, tears in her eyes. We spoke in French.

When I returned, I got out at Back Bay Station in Boston, thinking that I would stop at the public library on my way to my room. There were a few people in the old, battered train station, and among them, in his long overcoat and studying the board where arrivals and departures were displayed, was William, a Boston bag at his feet.

I stopped, he turned, and as he came toward me, I began to shake. He didn't speak, but his eyes were fixed on mine in a way that made me fix on his, and though I was shaking, I felt motionless. He reached out, and, my coat open on my shirt, he inserted a finger under a button to touch the flesh of my chest.

I asked him to come to my room, just for an hour. He leaned toward me as if to kiss me and, nodding, smiled. I said I didn't want him to think I was imposing myself on him, and he said, softly, that I was not imposing on him.

There, standing in the train station, he unbuttoned a button on my shirt.

In the taxi, I shook more, the shaking giving way to sudden shudders of my shoulders and legs. William didn't look at me, but out the side window at the falling snow.

With his bag, he followed me through the wet snow up the wooden steps to the porch and to the outside door, which had an oval window in it and a net curtain stretched over the glass. He followed me inside and up the stairs with rubber treads tacked to them to the narrow hallway of bare floorboards. And while I unlocked the door to my room, William stood beside me. When both of us were inside, I closed the door and turned to William. He dropped his bag and grabbed the sleeves of my overcoat in his fists and pulled at them.

He was sitting in the middle of the bed, from which the sheets and blankets had been pulled off so the mattress was bare, and I, behind him, was leaning against his back, my chin resting on the nape of his neck. We were rocking back and forth. The cast-iron radiator made the room warm, but there was a chill about the edges.

William became still and asked if he had had his gloves when he'd come in.

I said they were in the pocket of his overcoat, and I pressed against him to make him rock back and forth with me.

But William wouldn't move. He said he had to go to New York.

I asked if he had an appointment there.

He said he had a job, and he had to. But he stopped talking.

I, urging him with the movement of my body, made William move with me, back and forth.

He said, "This isn't what we are on earth for."

I said, "I believe that it is."

You see, there are no graphics to describe making love, none, all attempts fail as descriptions of disjointed sex. The sense of wholeness was possible, I knew, even for the details of sweat, smells, the guttural utterances that only occurred in sex. There was no describing that sense, however forced, if it was not experienced. It was not known but among us poor, pathetic human beings in our rank and rutting selves. It could only be known in the thrall of making love with the sense of wholeness that is love, love that reconciled all differences, all accidents, into one unifying essence of eternal love.

This is what I remember.

You are right to think that, writing this, I've made sex into something that only rarely occurs between lovers, and that in the recounting there most likely appears the banal, the bathetic sentiment of, yes, a fantasist. But I take the risk of a fantasy philosophy, because there is no unifying essence, free of differences and accidents, on which the philosophy of wholeness depends. And this I grieve.

William would sometimes fall away from me to lie separately and, even in the dark, I saw his eyes were open. I let him lie separate from me as long as he did, but I watched him closely, always expecting that he would suddenly rise and leave me. But he turned toward me, and he, not I, reached out to hold me and I felt all his long, firm, moist body pressed against mine.

And, however incidental to this narrative, I want to note that we were aware that we were both male. I was drawn to him with passion for a world that was a world of men. There is no accounting for this, which might very well have been an aberration because there was no reason in nature for it; and it might well have been because of a weakness in some men, because they were helpless in their attraction to one another. Two men making love is an act of mutual helplessness, for we cannot help but make love with one of our own.

And there is something more I want to write about the attraction of men to one another in a club where all are of the same sex, something I remember when I was young and went to those clubs, something beyond sexual attraction, something promised among men that not even sex would release. That sense of something emanated through the clothes of another you did not know, but who had the same sense of you through your clothes, both of you separated—in the shadows and shifting red spotlights of the club—from a world outside, where you felt safe to be among your kind. Everyone there was beautiful, everyone there embodied everything that beauty attracted, as if nothing else mattered but the beauty, to be revealed, oh yes, beneath the clothes in the body. And sometimes it happened that the connection was made, with the sudden certainty that you were beautiful enough, and on the way to his or your place, however incidental to all the talk, you felt that everything was right in the world, everything that was promised would be released. Perhaps you had never been as happy, or, at least, as free to express all that was in you to express. And, without resorting to any detailed depictions—which, anyway, would demean the fact in the grotesque details—there was, in a bedroom, by a bed already exposed to its sheets and pillows, the slow and amazing revelation of another body, and the amazing, even shocking, embrace of you and the other, chest against chest, thighs against thighs, sex against sex, that seemed never to have happened before, and would never happen again, you and he with arms held so tightly about each other that you could have been one. Oh yes, oh yes, youth and beauty rose up in the attraction, in the sudden vision you had of him, and you felt he had that of you, each of you in bed drawn back to look at each other with the wonder that you were both males, that this was very very strange, that this did not happen in the outside world, that we were extraordinary in making love to each other. And there was that moment to bring you together in a mutuality that made you so helplessly vulnerable to each other that sex must be, finally, love, when we both uttered a cry together, and then remained, lax, in each other's arms.

Three.

I was writing a novel, and on Friday and Saturday evenings, when I heard others calling to one another from the stairwell to hurry up to go out wherever they were going, to do whatever they planned to do together, I sat at an old table and worked on a novel.

And because the act of writing is important in this narrative, something from far enough in the past that it seems to me to come from another life that still holds me to it for all that it promised, all that was finally fulfilled as much as I dared to hope for fulfilment, I like to recall my ambitions as a writer then—ambitions, I have to make clear, that were about the writing itself. I wanted my writing to draw on the great past writers. I wanted references, however undetected by a reader, to the writing of those novelists I most admired. Among those writers, whom I now name because he eventually became a person who in fact appears in this novel, was E.M. Forster.

I liked his ability, in his very unassuming manner, to make memorable such delights as the sudden appearance and sudden disappearance of a pool in a verdant valley in which young naked men splashed about for fun. He could bring to the surface of his writing what had to have been to him a fantasy but that he made incidental in the very writing of it, and the seemingly incidental made it memorable. That was it—his way of making the seemingly incidental memorable. He could do that with the sudden death of a character in a sentence.

If I was to write about sex, I would try to do so in that way. My ambition was to write about sex more openly than any of the writers whose work I admired, but in no way graphically, because any sex described in its graphic details left out the sensation of it, the sense of it that was more than the details, that indescribable sense that comes with holding someone naked in your arms against your naked body.

I, alone in my room, was aware that the students who were out for a Friday or Saturday night were out for sex with more openness than I had known, given I was a generation older than they were, and, at their age, had been among those who had opened the world of sex for them, because I was of the generation that had acted on the fantasies that became expectations for the younger; I had had my Fridays and Saturdays of sex with young men met in bars in Boston, where, to enter there, was to be free, if not in the world outside.

In there, ironically (and irony had a lot to do with being inside), we were protected from the policing of the outside by the Boston mafia inside. The mafia were our friends, and we were friends of the mafia. We knew that, and we enjoyed being lawless. I thought, the younger generation were now within the law.

The world of sex I had lived in had had its writers, but none of them was an E.M. Forster; they allowed, as given, descriptions of sex that in no way appeared incidental. No doubt it was in my disposition that, as much as I did enjoy the sense of freedom of a young man having sex in men's rooms in New York subway stations, the fantasy of it all was too obviously fantasy, and the more graphic the sex the more exposed as fantasy.

But it might easily happen that I would drop my pen to the gutter if I carried along the notebook in which I wrote late on a Friday or Saturday night. I recall myself mostly wearing white broadcloth, button-down collar shirts and knit ties and corduroy suits and loafers. I walked down the side of Beacon Hill away from Back Bay, almost to the elevated highway, to go to a bar called Sporters. The spring afternoon was bright. The façade and windows of Sporters were painted black, and the inside, too, was painted black, with spotlights in the dark. I ordered a beer. There weren't many men in the bar, and most of them were playing pool at the back. Leaning on a post and swigging from my bottle, I watched them. One was bare-chested, his tee shirt dangling from his belt. I pulled down the knot of my tie and unbuttoned my collar, then wandered in the dimness. Beyond the beam of a spotlight stood a guy on his own. I hesitated before I walked around the light and looked. He was wearing a blue working man's shirt, the sleeves rolled up to his elbows, and construction worker's boots. As if he were searching the place for someone he'd come to meet, the guy looked everywhere else but at me, though I kept my eyes on him, and when the guy did look toward me, I fixed his look on my own. The guy was blond, with a smooth blond face and neck, and he smiled. I didn't smile back, but, walking behind the guy, touched his shoulder lightly, then I put my empty bottle on the bar and went out into the sunlight. Climbing back up the hill, I asked myself why I had done that, and I told myself to go back, but I continued to my room.

I wanted to write about that experience in the novel.

It was in me, yes, it was, to look for experience to write about it.

And there was William.

When I thought of William as belonging to another world, I imagined him as a Yankee, which meant he was of a history that had become the history of America, whereas my history had failed in America.

All he ever told me about his family was that on New Year's Eve, members gathered in his grandmother's house with printed chronologies of their relationships and the amusement was to find out who was related to whom, and how. But I could not imagine them, not in his grandmother's house, how many they were, what they looked like, how they were dressed, and I relied on images received from history, though I was sure that if I had been there, the images would not have applied, and what I had imagined was nothing like what it actually was.

Nor, I supposed, could he have known my history, and if he had any idea, it would have been his idea of the world I came from: that of French history in North America, la Nouvelle France. He would have known because there were references to us in Yankee history, that we should be treated in New England, if not as equals, then with respect, even if, in the vast history of North America, we were a defeated people. We were defeated by the English, from whose colonial conquest of the French in North America he might have thought he had inherited a legitimate possession of all the continent, and certainly New England, which made him legitimate, and the French not legitimate.

Yankees could claim the arrival on the *Mayflower*. The French might have claimed the arrival, decades earlier, of Champlain, if they had known about Champlain, but they were disconnected from their history in the then Nouvelle France. And it was not to their advantage in a Yankee world that the French could refer backwards to an Indian ancestor, nor that Indians had fought with the French against the English in the war for the continent.

I liked to think that William could not have placed me in my past history in the parochial school's classroom where a nun shouted out when a bird flew in by an open window, *C'est le diable!*

I had my own history.

But there was this: his beauty was, to me, Yankee beauty.

There was hardly more to our friendship than making love, and there we were equal, because sex made us equal when we were in bed in a bedroom in an old apartment house, where coal dust from long past heating was impacted in the cracks between the old floorboards.

I don't know if he thought that to have sex was why we were on earth, but it was as though he had been sent to me to fulfill that blessing. He appeared often enough shortly after I returned from the language school where I taught English to foreigners, and if we did have a drink of whiskey to start us off, it was to kiss and pour into each other's mouth. The whiskey dribbled down our chins as we kissed.

And how do I evoke—because that is the impulse, to evoke—the sex between us? No, not graphically, no—and yet, how? In retrospect, after many years, this was what I wanted to do even as we shifted positions so our bodies slid against each other: wanted to evoke the very spirit of sex.

I remember this: he, lying by my side, his eyes closed, and I, propped up on an elbow, looking down at him, looking at his naked body exposed to me for my pleasure, for my great pleasure. Sometimes I lightly ran a finger down his chest to his cock that stirred a little and he smiled.

We had that, we had in my recollection the full fantasies of sex, with a little extra titillation when he tickled me, and I giggled uncontrollably.

He did not stay for a simple supper in my room, nor did we go out together to a restaurant, and nor did we ever go to a bar together, or meet at a bar we had gone to separately, all we had was that wonderful sex in my bed.

He dressed and went off, and I got up and, in my underpants, ate a sandwich at the table where I worked on the novel that I imagined evolved in ways that included him in Boston, where, it seemed to me, we could have a fictional relationship that included sex.

On a sunny evening and walking from the language school in Back Bay through the Public Gardens and the Boston Common on my way to my room on Beacon Hill, I was aware of sex in the bodies of young people lying on grass, but it occurred to me I only wanted to have sex with William. And this, I knew, was because he was beautiful.

I was not really promiscuous because sexual attraction for me had to be to someone I saw as beautiful, and perhaps the beauty I looked for was rare enough that, even in a bar, I held myself back from being looked at, and when I looked at someone I found beautiful, he mostly looked away.

I wondered in what way there was in my history, in which the devil was so present, an exemption from the devil in sex that made sex so wonderful. That exemption, I thought, must have come from my religion, my Roman Catholic religion, and there was enough belief in that religion, as primitive as it was, in the mystical body.

Five.

I had friends in Boston, especially a couple who had bought a very run-down townhouse in Rutland Square when that neighborhood was inhabited by drunkards who lived in squalor and all night threw bottles from windows that crashed onto the pavements below; but more and more, people bought, and more and more the townhouses in the square were restored, and at night the windows were lit up to reveal curtains and framed pictures on the walls.

I had met William there.

The last time he came to me, he spent the night, so I slept with his body in my arms, but we didn't make love. In the morning, he got up and I heard him showering in the bathroom, from where he emerged, drying himself with a towel, and then he stood by the bed and dropped the towel, his gleaming body exposed, and he asked me, "Do you love me?" I stared at his beautiful body as if my answer would have to do with that, with my loving his shoulders, his chest, his thighs, his sex, his legs, and his arms, his hands held out to me.

Gently, I said, "No."

How could I love him? I didn't know him, not even enough to have his address or even a telephone number, as his coming was always up to him.

And yet, time after time, the wonder was why the most intimate act of making love was not consummate with love, or at least a familiarity with each other that was as close as it was possible for two people to be together even when sitting on separate armchairs and talking about the weather.

I said, "I love your body when we make love."

He nodded, as if that was enough for him to know.

I lay in bed after he had gone, and I knew he would not come again, and a sense came to me of having been abandoned, a sense of something that was so important to me I would find its absence difficult.

That sense of something went out with him and I found it a strain to get up and get ready to go to the language school.

My student that morning was a middle-aged Italian man. I could not confirm for him that in English one didn't simply say, "rains," or "snows," or one didn't say "makes dark out," but "it is raining," or "it is snowing," and one says, "it is dark out," and I began myself to wonder what that "it" refers to, what is "it" that is raining or snowing, what is that "it" that is dark out?

After my last class, I went, uninvited (but I knew they would welcome me with embraces) to my friends, the lovers who had a house in Rutland Square, and, as I often did, I asked to sleep between them for the reassurance that I felt I needed, and I can say that there is nothing more reassuring than to sleep soundly between two lovers in their bed.

All the time I had free I wrote at an old table on an old chair, working on the novel set in my French parish in Providence, as if where I was born and brought up had to be saved by the novel. I did not think there was any other novel written that had been set there.

From my grandmother, I had learned that on a certain day of the year, water was curative, and if on that day rain fell, she went out into the backyard to stand in it until her long dress was wet. That I didn't know where that belief came from made it all the stranger, because my father's mother was in part Indian, her grandmother of the Pied-noir confederacy tribe.

My mother, having been educated not in the parish grammar school, but in a primary public school, liked to read the books in English that I brought home from the library. For a student in high school who didn't know French and was assigned a passage from the novel *Atala* by Chateaubriand, she did the translation of the passage on the death of the Indian, and she praised the beauty of the story as well as the beauty of the French.

All of this I wanted to possess in my writing, the getting it down, I felt, the historical permanence of it, the publishing incidental—incidental because I knew nothing of publishing, nothing.

I kept to myself the subject matter of what I was writing about, when, in Rutland Square at a party my friends often gave, I did say I was writing a novel but stopped when I was asked, did I have an agent? And there was nothing I could recount about the novel that would have been interesting to anyone there, for never did I meet a Franco, as we were called; and if I had, I would not have wanted him to know I was a Franco, too.

The talk was about sex, and that I could engage in—if not to the extravagance of someone recounting his going to the Fens park behind the Museum of Fine Arts where he met someone with a pecker, oh, that big, and opened his hands for the size. I enjoyed this talk. Everyone there was in the same world of sex and, yes, there was a great spontaneity in our talk that sometimes led to someone coming to my room for the night, or my going to the bedroom of someone I had met there. I recall a large brass bed.

On a weekend back in the Providence parish, I went to Mass with my parents, because they would have been upset by a son whose life apart from them they could not imagine, and going to Mass with them reassured them.

I noted that there was a hole in one of the stained-glass windows, and there were very few congregated, and of these old parishioners at Mass.

Kneeling to pray, there came to me the idea that the parish had become a palisaded fortress holding itself off from the world outside; and as I thought about this I found that the idea of the palisaded fortress as my parish was very much in keeping with our history, for it was as though we had begun our French colonies in forts, far back when we were the first to make our lives on the vast continent, and we had failed in our efforts in the outside because to be in the fort closed in by the trunks of pine trees felled in the forest was to be as much as we could ever be. There would have been a Native woman among us, because we had always found something noble in Indians, however savage the English colonists found them. And when the time came, perhaps because the land a Franco farmed did not yield enough for them, or perhaps houses were foreclosed, or perhaps the outside became threatening, they moved with the fort enclosing them, those forts that had once been garrisons along the great rivers of the continent, and they stayed in their forts until a hole broke through the stained-glass window of their church, until the timbers of the palisade began to fall apart, and we became ghosts in the idea of our once holding our own in our forts.

A Sunday afternoon of snow, I couldn't write because I was restless and I went, as I often did, to my friends in Rutland Square because I knew that on a Sunday afternoon when snow fell there seemed nothing else to do but meet friends.

I rang the bell to one of the couples living there. But on opening, my friend kept me back for a moment, his tone as though to warn me: "William is here."

That I should be warned made me wonder what he knew of the relationship I had had with William, because I had, as he'd wished, kept it to myself.

"And?" I asked.

"He's with someone, an Englishman, a poet."

Seven.

The poet was named Cecil.

I confess now that if not nostalgia, some sense of the past distorts the narrative of this account of my life. Not that I want to relive that past, because of course that can't be, but to allow what didn't quite happen to have happened in this novel.

There was a fire in the old, ornate fireplace, and there was an ornate tea that the lovers had evidently served William and the poet Cecil on the low table set within reach of the armchairs and sofa and fringed hassocks. But now that I was there, they left and one of them brought in a cup for me and indicated the cake on its cake stand and plates and silver forks for me to help myself, and then he left, as if he and his absent lover thought there was something to be resolved among those remaining, snow falling against the bay windows with fringed curtains in swags. William and I glanced at one another, but nothing was said.

As the poet spoke, however, I felt a note of sadness in his voice. If not sadness, an acceptance that he had had to make of the world as it was and that was not his, for he was, to me, large, with big hands and big shoes, as though he had never quite found the right proportions to live in a world that he wanted to accept him. I learned that this was also the way with his poetry, sensitive but not quite accepted for its sensitivity.

His way of talking about English poets that I had merely read about was that his knowing them was incidental to him, a way of talking I later learned was very English, because the more known in the world writers were, the more incidental knowing them, often as if not quite recalling them, even touching a forehead to try to recall. Well, yes, he did know E.M. Forster, he said without my asking but knowing I wanted to know that he did, his knowing rather incidental to him, as he liked me to think.

The poet had not only met, he knew E.M. Forster and often went to visit him where he lived in King's College, Cambridge, though Forster sometimes went to stay with a married couple, the husband a former lover of Morgan, as Cecil called Forster.

I tried to make my interest incidental when I said, "I once heard that Forster has written an unpublished novel."

"Yes, he has."

"You've read it?"

"Yes, I have. It is called *Maurice*."

"Why hasn't it been published?"

"A number of reasons, and at least one of them is reasonable. It's not terribly good."

"Oh?"

"It should be, it's about two undergraduates at King's who fall in love, and Morgan should know something about that."

"Why isn't is good?"

"It's more fantasy than not. I don't think Morgan has ever truly been in love, but fantasizes about it. I think that when he says it shouldn't be published, he is really worried that it won't ring true, not when he calls sex 'sharing' and at midnight, he puts out a ladder for a gardener to climb up to an open window where a man is waiting to share with him, arms open.

"In fact," the poet said, "when you think about it, there is a lot of fantasy about sex in Forster's novels. That couldn't be otherwise, given the time he wrote his novels. I suppose the times now are more accepting, aren't they?"

I felt this was a way of asking me if I was accepting. I said, "Yes, they are."

"Still," he said, "there are lovely lines in the novel, yes, lovely," and he said, as a matter of fact, "his friend filled him with beauty and taught him tenderness."

I was touched by this quotation, and it came to me that I liked the poet very much for that beautiful line.

He asked me, "How old are you?"

"Twenty-five."

"Ah, twenty-five! And I suspect you are a writer, are you not?"

"I haven't been published. I don't have an agent, and wouldn't know how to engage one."

"You are a writer if you write."

"Well, thank you."

William said, "It is getting late," and he stood, and I had the sense that he took offense to the intimacy between the poet and me, along with the sense that I wasn't up to that intimacy, that I wasn't up to William at all in the world, and that he would not have introduced me to Cecil, the English poet, and had done so only because I had come on my own on this winter Sunday afternoon.

William went out to find the lovers, and I sat on the sofa with the poet, and I could not think of anything to say, nor, I felt, could he.

I thought I would not see William again, that sense of something not resolved among him and Cecil the poet and me reason enough for him to stay away. But I never did know him well enough to want to understand him and his relationship with me.

That same evening, I was about to go to bed when he rang the outside bell to my room and when he entered, in an aura of winter chill, he drew me to him and he commanded me with kisses, pressing me to a wall and hardly pausing in his kissing as he threw off his hat, his coat, his scarf, and unbuttoned his shirt as he unbuttoned the jacket of my pajamas.

And there he was, William as I loved him, naked, and I naked and pressed against him.

Whatever was unresolved between William and me, which I was not interested in enough to wonder at, its resolution was in sex, as passionate as sex could be, our bodies made sensitive by the rough stubble of our beards.

He did not spend the night. Leaving, he told me that the poet, Cecil, would like to meet me again.

I had read the poet's memoir, *Worlds Within Worlds*. And for me to read about people I had only ever fantasized about—W.H. Auden, Christopher Isherwood, Stephen Spender, and the inner world of the Bloomsbury group, which included Virginia Woolf and Leonard Woolf and Vita Sackville-West and Vanessa Bell and Duncan Grant and Lytton Strachey and Lady Ottoline Morrell and T.S. Eliot and E.M Forster, all of whom Cecil in fact knew—was to open up that world, that entirely English world, in which I fantasized having a place, even if that world no longer existed in itself. It existed in the witness of Cecil.

And Bloomsbury became a world to me in the novels I read—a novel that held me in the thrall of Mrs. Dalloway arranging a large bouquet of flowers in a vase and Mrs. Ramsay reading and Lily Briscoe painting at an easel and Percival listening to the sea waves with a shell to an ear. And characters from another writer appeared. On a little pool made by rainwater, naked, splashing one another, are Mr. Beebe, George, and Freddy. One of the trees is a wych elm, and by it sits Helen Schlegel, writing a letter and hearing someone sneezing, "a tissue, a tissue!" And somewhere beyond the trees, in an open space, a cricket match is being played.

It was as though I was nostalgic for a world that I in no way lived in except in the novels set in that world, a world that could not be more different than the world I was baptized and grew up in.

My fantasy of England, as inspired by Bloomsbury, was this: that it was a country of respect for differences in each and every one, all the more so for the startling originality of each and every one. This respect was made possible because they all knew one another, all of them, and they all knew that they had created in their work a new awareness that was English, whatever the Englishness of the awareness could be.

I fantasized myself, say, at high table at King's College Cambridge, with Maynard Keynes presiding, I at one side of him and at the other Rupert Brooke, and after there would be wine in Maynard Keynes's rooms with Dadie Rylands and Virginia Woolf and E.M. Forster, talking about—well, talking about everyone that they knew, talking about them, however critically, with a sense that they made up a world. And they did make up a world, and they knew that the world was English. And they all slept with one another.

But, I had to remind myself, this was my fantasy of a world of writers, and I had no idea if it had anything at all to do with England.

Nine.

I moved to London because of Cecil.

I am trying to make this transition interesting, at least in the writing of it, if I can. I do not want to rely on names to make it so, in the way I rely on the name E.M. Forster for interest. I would prefer everyone in this narrative to be an invention because that would be in keeping with the invention of narrative, which is to me the invention of writing, because if this novel is about anything that can be claimed as its deepest interest, that would be the art of writing.

I lived with Cecil in the small house he had in Kensington, from where we often walked to Hyde Park on afternoons. In the way the friends whom he introduced me to seemed to embrace me with total acceptance of my living with Cecil, our relationship simply didn't exist apart from the social world, I sometimes wondered if it did exist when Cecil and I were alone at home together, where he was as attentive to me as he was when we were at a drinks party, as if his graciousness to me in private was his graciousness to others at the party. It was understood, without any evidence to it, that Cecil was in love with me and I was in love with him, and that we were a couple, to be invited together, and the understanding in no way needed any example to make it a matter of fact, for the fact was self-evident in our being known as a couple.

This was particularly evident at luncheons at the restaurant Chez Victor. I learned the restaurant had been a meeting place for the London writers and artists, so renowned that there was a painting that commemorated the usual people who gathered there, with Ezra Pound opening a door to enter and be greeted by friends crowded at a table. And though I was very much of a younger generation than the generation younger than that of Ezra Pound, I liked to think I had my place there, the young American who was writing a novel. That was all that was needed to be known about me to be there, because I was there with Cecil, who always introduced me as a writer, and that was reason enough for me to be with him.

And nothing was asked of my past in America, though the novel I was writing was about that past, that palisaded parish about which, even had I been asked, there wouldn't have been enough knowledge for me to place it in British history; and the defeat of the French by the English on the Plains of Abraham in Quebec was only interesting to me in London because I, French, had been defeated by the English, among whom I was making my living, helped by the Englishman Cecil, who introduced me to his publishing friends for whom I wrote reports on books being considered or I translated from the French. And he introduced me to an agent.

I would rather keep our love for each other as it was accepted at the restaurant Chez Victor, accepted by the writer Joe Ackerly, whom Cecil invited to lunch for me to meet him and ask how Morgan Forster was, because Ackerly saw Forster often and would be able to tell us, in preparation of Cecil taking me to King's College, Cambridge, if Forster was well enough.

I was always aware of my moment of acceptance or not, but Ackerly didn't talk to me, he talked to Cecil about people I knew nothing about but, again, names—I did dare to tell him when there was a pause in the conversation between the men, "Cecil told me you wrote a book about a dog."

Ignoring me, Ackerly said to Cecil, "Morgan is well enough for you to visit him," which seemed to leave me out, but he did look at me and said, "He likes meeting young men, Forster does," and this seemed to forgive me for having seemingly accused him of having written a book about a dog.

And there was this, that whenever I saw, in the lobby of a theater, in a shop, on the street, a beautiful young man—young because I was aging enough to think of the young as separate from me—the sense came over me that I have to call love. Yes, I loved him, and I loved him for his beauty, and beauty appeared to be his sex, the sex of the beautiful.

Ten.

I made friends with people of my age.

One, named Mark, invited me to go with him to a club, and would drive me there. In the back seat of the automobile sat three sisters close together—Henrietta and Amaryllis and Fanny Garnett, all, I think, the daughters of Angelica Bell, the daughter of Vanessa Bell, the sister of Virginia Woolf, as Mark had explained to me. He had also explained that Henrietta was married to Burgo Partridge, the son of Frances and Ralph Partridge, with whom—Ralph, that is—Lytton Strachey had been in love. And to complicate it all, Ralph Partridge, before Frances, had been in love with Dora Carrington, who, out of her impossible love for Lytton Strachey, killed herself. Mark took us all to a queer club, which, in the early afternoon, was empty except for us. Mark and I sat at a table and watched the three sisters, all in long dresses with embroidery across the bodices and even longer scarves, dance together, their clothes swinging.

Days later, Mark rang me to tell me that Amaryllis drowned herself in the Thames.

From Liverpool Street Station, Cecil and I trained to Cambridge, where we had lunch in a simple restaurant, and after I followed him through the massive gate of King's College, where there was a sign in various languages that only the Fellows of the college were allowed to walk on the grass on the front courtyard, and past a heavy door and up some stone steps to a door, and he knocked.

A delicate voice said, "Come in, come in."

E.M. Forster, short and bent, was in his shirt sleeves. "I've just seen the doctor," he said. "I've just seen the doctor."

"Are you well?" Cecil asked.

"Oh, indeed, indeed."

Cecil introduced us, and when I shook Forster's hand, I imagined shaking hands—as if all their handshakes remained like hundreds of invisible hands about his—with Virginia Woolf, with Maynard Keynes, with Lytton Strachey, with all of Bloomsbury, and, extending even more out into the world, with Constantine Cavafy in Alexandria. He went into his bedroom to put on his jacket and on the way out shut the door of his bathroom, where I saw a long, claw-footed Victorian tub that listed.

We sat before his fireplace, above which were oil paintings and, I gathered, family photographs. The furniture was all Victorian, rather old-maidenish, with knitted arm covers on the chairs. High bookcases, with big yellow and brown books, lined the walls one after another like large rectangular librarians standing at attention. The wallpaper was of yellow stripes and vague flowers. One of the oil paintings, all in vivid yellow, red, and green, was of King's chapel done by an undergraduate, another a mountain scene by Roger Fry, and on a wall between the bedroom and bathroom was a reproduction of Picasso's young naked man leading a horse.

Pointing at me, Cecil said, "He told Joe he had heard he'd written a book about a dog," and he smiled.

"Joe bores me about his dogs," E.M. Forster said. "He does bore me about his dogs."

He paused for long periods between sentences, and seemed always to repeat what he said.

He said he had painted the bottom panes of the windows of the room so he wouldn't have to see the ugly modern building, the Keynes Building, across the way.

Cecil talked of the latest news, some minor colonels in Greece had imposed a dictatorship on the country.

Yes, E.M. Forster said, he had heard, he had heard, and he was deeply upset that a dictatorship should be imposed on Greece, on Greece, especially.

He thought for a moment.

"I do love Greece, yes, I do, and I believe the love of Greece is deep in us, I do, and so it is, yes, that Greece is so deep in us that we are deeply Greek, and, yes, it is very disturbing that all that Greece means to us is now . . ." But he didn't continue, and raised a hand, blinking while thinking, and he said, "But, you see, I have been many places, many, in the world, that were deeply meaningful to me, deeply so. So much so that when I was there I was pleased to be there, though, even when I was there, there was every reason not to be pleased because, well, of everything going on around one that was not at all pleasant, and should have been reason enough to leave."

E.M. Forster lowered his head and looked down, then raised his head.

He said, "Somehow one's dearest memories are of events that, if one saw them in the world, were always embedded in muck."

Cecil said, "I don't doubt that."

"Wherever you go, your dearest memories from there have always been embedded in muck that you thought had nothing to do with you, but that had everything to do with you," E.M. Forster said.

"I would have thought a stay on Mount Athos would have been pleasant," Cecil said.

I knew about Mount Athos, the Greek peninsula of all-male monasteries where, supposedly, not even hens were allowed, and I supposed Cecil liked to make a little joke of it to please E.M. Forster that only men lived there, a very little joke.

Forster said he'd once been on a boat that was on an excursion to the Halkediki but that stopped at Mount Athos. "The men got off," he said quietly, "but I stayed onboard with the ladies."

After twenty minutes, Cecil said he had to get back to London, so we left.

I did not remember that E.M. Forster had said anything to me.

On the train, Cecil commented, "There was a lot of Forster in that remark about one's dearest memories always being embedded in muck."

"Oh?"

"The horrors of the world enclosing our most meaningful moments of life."

I had never known from anyone else the loving care I had received from Cecil, and now that he is dead for some twenty years, I know that he was the only person in my life whom I loved, and who I knew loved me, as we were in our individual selves, because he always respected my individuality, even helped me and praised my writing.

And I think that there is nothing to reveal about our love but that it was accepted by everyone we knew, for as I was more and more accepted by London, or the London that consisted of everyone knowing one another, I found that I was able, at a dinner party, to talk about people known mutually, and among the people known mutually, the love that Cecil and I had for each other became a fact of the ever interconnecting mutuality.

And if this surprised me a little because the law was then that our love for each other was unlawful, especially considering the difference in our ages, for he was thirty years older than I was, the surprise gave way to the world of mutuality that we lived in. I do not want to name names to give this world its history, because there is only to mention that when someone of that world was sentenced for seducing a boy he met in Piccadilly Circus and invited home, a boy scout, a very aged friend named Charlotte announced at dinner, "Those terrible, terrible boy scouts, they should be disbanded." Cecil and I were not going to seduce boy scouts.

Charlotte was perhaps our dearest friend, and, yes, there was a mutuality I shared when at our very simple dinners, prepared by us in the kitchen and served by us, Charlotte told her stories, which were not for approval, or so I thought, but for the amusements of past history, as when, on a visit with the British governor of a past colony and being driven in his open car along a highway where the Natives bowed as the car passed, she asked, why were they bowing? And he responded, their black bottoms would be very red if they didn't, and everyone at the table laughed, and there was irony in the laugh, and indulgence.

As for my being American, I very much liked to recount Charlotte once asking me, "You're American, aren't you?" And when I answered that I was, she, leaning toward me, asked, "Do you know the Roosevelts?"

Cecil was not gentry, though he had a brother who was a member of the House of Lords, and his brother and his wife came to supper in the kitchen, with pots from the cooker on the table, at which she exclaimed, as if it were a rallying cry, "Pots on the table!"

I published the novel I had been working on for a long time about my parish, and I tried to include in it such stories that might have been told at table, because Cecil did tell stories and I did in emulation of him, learning that it was what one did at a table, told stories. And he and the others deferred to mine until my story of my great grandmother wearing a bearskin did not fit in, and I told the story of having sat next to a woman on a bus who told me that she had just divorced her husband, and she had because she couldn't bear insisting the Royal Family were Hanoverian German, to which someone at the table said, but they were! My novel was a success in America, but not in Britain.

Cecil had a slim volume of his poetry published, and the publishing house gave a party, though he did not expect more, the reviews did group him with other poets of his generation, and admired the poised sentiment of his poems.

He was liked and I, with him, was liked.

There was a memorial service for him in Saint Martin in the Fields in Trafalgar Square, and on the porch, from where the fountains were seen gushing, I was approached by friends, including his brother and sister-in-law and their grown children, and I was embraced and told that I must come to the reception to be held in their house in Saint John's Wood. But I asked to be excused, and they understood, because they would have sensed that without him, I did not belong.

Even though I had become British, and my books were reviewed in the British weeklies, and I had assumed a certain London pronunciation in saying *category*, I felt I was exposed to being, not American, but not anyone, for I had become Cecil, and he was gone. It seemed to me I had no nationality.

Alone in the small house that had become as much mine as it had been his, I wondered, after having lived in London for forty years, if I should go, not back to Boston, but to somewhere Cecil and I had been happy together—to Greece, where we had a house on the island of Aegina, and if, even there, the memories of being happy were embedded in muck that should have not made the memories happy, we had been happy enough, sitting out on the terrace drinking ouzo and eating the pistachios the island was famous for, for we were, Cecil and me, always happy enough, and if I write *we were always loving towards one another enough*, the *enough* held itself against the muck, held itself against the muck of infidelities, of deceits, of betrayals, even of doubts, and I owed it to Cecil, and owe it still, that he was able to sustain and help me to sustain the purest love I believed possible.

Thirteen.

On the day I was appointed to arrive at King's College Cambridge for an interview that may or may not have led to my position there as writer-in-residence, I went, after the interview, to the Fitzwilliam Museum.

In the museum, all my attention was centered, not on any work of art, but on a young man. I won't try to describe him except to say he was beautiful. I followed him from room to room, and stopped at a distance from him when he stopped to study a picture.

I followed him into the gallery of Roman and Greek antiquities, the broken torsos displayed among fluted columns. He had stopped before, yes, a Greek statue, and I, a fool, hurried ahead to stop with him to study the broken marble statue of a youth, the slim torso in the subtle counterpoised position, one hip higher than the other, one delicate foot placed before the other on the marble plinth.

He turned away and I was too embarrassed now to follow him, as if he knew of my fantasy and would in no way indulge me in it.

I thought, for all that I fantasized about making love to him, the greater fantasy I had was of the marble statue, for it appeared to me that the statue, even broken, was closer to how I saw the body of a young man, however beautiful, because the marble, dense, showed itself all outwardly, with no inner blood or bones or muscles, and was all that I wanted to make love with, which was the beauty of the body.

What was that sense the beauty of the body gave off?

Back in London, I was rung up and told that I had been accepted at King's College to be writer-in-residence.

In the museum, all my attention was centered, not on any work of art, but on a young man.

Fourteen.

When I went to the porters' lodge with my suitcase to take up residence, I was politely given the key to my rooms in the Keynes Building. This was the very building that caused Forster to have his windows painted so he wouldn't see it. I was told to go to the N staircase, which I then had to find. This wasn't rudeness. At King's, I discovered, you were left to create your own world.

As I was unpacking, a woman, wearing an apron and slippers with fake fur turndowns, knocked and came in. She was the bed maker, or bedder, and she told me she wouldn't be able to do my set as the Kingsman who had inhabited the set next to mine for many years had refused to allow her in, and now that he was gone she would have to do a big spring cleaning. I said my rooms looked clean, so she needn't worry, and then I asked her if she wouldn't mind coming just once a week, as I rather liked not being disturbed. I would make my own bed.

(Later, I learned that many undergraduates got out of their beds for the bedder to make them up, then got right back into them.)

Unpacked, I looked out my windows into Webbs Court, where I saw undergraduates, some pushing bicycles, hurrying back and forth, all knowing by long tradition just what to do in this cloistered world.

An American's fantasy of England couldn't have been more fulfilled than mine was by living at King's College.

In the evening, hungry, I thought I should go down to hall for a meal. As I descended worn stone steps, I noticed, on top of old wooden coal storage bins on the landings, trays with dirty plates. Wandering along passageways, I came to a room where Fellows were gathered, or I presumed, because of their academic gowns, that they were Fellows. I thought the only thing to do was to go in, and I entered the Senior Combination Room, the walls bright red in the electric light, with armchairs and sofas and a long table with magazines and newspapers spread across it, and portraits on the walls. Some Fellows were sitting alone, some were gathered in small groups, and I approached one of these and introduced myself.

An elderly man, a divine of the Church of England who had written books on the Eucharist, asked me, "Where is your gown? You must wear a gown, or we won't know who you are."

"I don't have a gown," I said.

"There are some hanging in the pantry, aren't there?" he asked the others.

"There should be," someone said laconically.

"But I'm not sure I'm entitled to have one," I said. "I'm not really a fellow."

"You have dining rights at high table, don't you?"

I said, "I think I do."

"Then you're entitled to, and *should*, wear a gown."

He told me he wasn't a fellow himself, didn't even live in College, but had dining rights, and I realized the rights were delicately complicated. I also quickly learned that all the ritualistic rights could be dispensed with simply by ignoring them, and no one would mind. Except perhaps the butler.

When he took me to the butler in the pantry to explain that I would be eating in, if that were possible, "Very well," the butler said. But he wasn't so forthcoming about the gown. He said, looking toward the ceiling, "Well, sir, I'm not sure the writer-in-residence is entitled to one."

"Of course he's entitled to one," the Divine said.

A gown was found for me, and the Divine and I went back into the Senior Combination Room. I noticed that some Fellows wore their gowns over sweaters and jeans.

The butler came in and opened the second of the double doors to the Combination Room and announced that dinner was served. At that point, the most senior Fellow there, who I had no idea what knowledge of my presence he had since he had been talking to a group of other Fellows, approached me and asked me if I'd sit next to him, and he led the small procession out, along a passageway with pictures of former Kingsmen on its walls. He was a great scholar of Persian poetry. He was Mr. Peter Avery, the title *Mr.* on a higher level than *Dr.*

He pointed to a small picture of a fat man in a brown suit, and said as we passed it, "That's Oscar Browning. There's a story about him that you might find amusing. He was with some undergraduates on a bank of the Cam, in which they'd all been swimming, starkers, of course, when a boatload of ladies came along. The undergraduates picked up their shirts and wrapped them around their waists. Oscar Browning wrapped his around his head. After the ladies passed, he said to the undergraduates, 'I don't know what you are known by around here, but I'm known by my face.' He was greatly loved."

Entering Hall, a long, narrow, high, neo-Gothic dining room with long tables, I noticed Fellows seem to try to get quickly to places at the table set for us and stand holding the backs of chairs, and I learned later that people who'd been conversing together in the Combination Room and who wanted to sit near one another at high table, had, on entering Hall, to rush, as decorously as possible, to places. If there were a lot of people dining, the places filled quickly, and you might be separated from the people with whom you'd hoped to go on conversing.

As we stood about the table in silence, the senior Fellow presiding said grace: "*Benedictus bendicat.*" We sat.

Along the table were silver bowls of flowers and large white napkins. And there was a printed menu.

Dinner

* * *

Asparagus Spears with Parma Ham

Black & Green Olives

Vinaigrette Dressing

* * *

Salmon & Brill Plait with Ginger

Waldorf Salad

Parisienne Potatoes

* * *

Exotic Fruit Salad & Cream

* * *

*

Fresh Fruit and Stilton Cheese available

Cairanne, Côtes du Rhônes Village,

Caves des Coteaux, DB, 1982

Macon Peronne, "Du Mortier,"

M. Josserand, DB, 1983

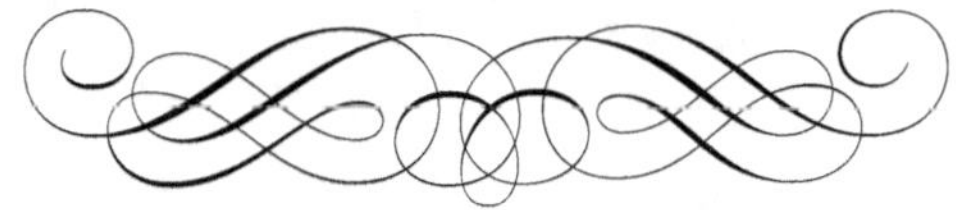

A Fellow told me that high table used to be at the other end of Hall, on a platform, which meant that the Fellows had had to process the length of the Hall, past the tables of the undergraduates who stood as if in ranks at their places.

But in the sixties, when everything changed, undergraduates protested against sitting at tables all together at a set time and being served; now they came in at any time and served themselves with trays cafeteria-style. The Fellows' high table was moved to the other end of Hall, next to the entrance from the Senior Common Room, and placed, no longer on a platform to make it high, but on the stone floor along with the tables of the undergraduates.

I saw, beyond the bobbing heads of the diners at high table, the undergraduates carrying their trays to and from the tables, and through the talk all about me I heard their distant, faintly echoing voices and the sounds of their knives and forks against their plates. high table seemed very far from them. A great tapestry—a gift, I was told, from Morgan (E.M. to me) Forster to the College—hung on the wall behind my back.

Having glanced about the table to make sure all the diners had finished eating, the senior Fellow rose, and everyone else did and stood still while he said, "*Deo gratias*." As people were dispersing, the senior Fellow said to me, "You've chosen a good day for your first dinner at high table. Tonight is wine night. Would you like to join us in the Wine Room?"

Every Tuesday and Thursday after dinner, those who wanted were invited into a special room for wine on the

College. Under a chandelier was a large, bright table, and on it were dishes of dried fruit and nuts and clementines. A little silver train, in the carriages of which were decanters of after-dinner wines that clinked together, was pulled round the table to the left—never to the right—from person to person. The different-sized glasses appropriate to the different wines were at one's place, but it didn't really matter which glass one used for what wine.

The silver train went round and round, eventually, it seemed, on its own steam. The butler ended the wine night with passing round cigarettes (gratis) or cigars (non-gratis) and coffee.

There were moments when the rituals seemed totally dispensable and in the hands, if in any, not of the Fellows, but the butler. And I thought that if he suddenly stopped announcing dinner and opening the double doors, if the silver and flowers disappeared from the table, no one would really object.

Would it matter, I wondered, if grace were never said? Would it matter if no one wore gowns, which, in any case, were only half worn, slipping off shoulders, and in the case of an old one, living in bachelor don, frayed and shiny green with age? Though no one seemed to care, there was, always, the invisible presence of the rituals, as if maintained, even more than by the butler, by invisible people, generation upon generation of them, who sat about the table with us, more sensitive to us than we were to them. Encircled by them, high table seemed to float in the vast dimness of Hall. Sometimes the table floated off entirely, up above dark Cambridge, then, along with the clouds, in the direction of the prevailing wind, and no one seemed to notice.

Some days later, I went to the college library, where the head librarian slowed me what Forster had meant to be the last chapter of *Maurice*, thought to be too sentimentally improbable to publish. In the chapter, as I recall, Maurice's sister, on a stroll, catches a glimpse of her brother and his now lover living together happily in the woods. I thought how the men of that generation had had a vision of love that had to have been improbable because they hadn't lived the reality of the love. Forster appeared to me to have been a man of innocence, and I felt a sense of tenderness towards him for what he had, however gently, longed for.

I also read letters to Oscar Browning in the college collection.

This was from a schoolboy protégé, Ernest Barrett: "We played the King's Lynn Policemen at cricket this afternoon & beat them by 133 runs." Or: "I am sorry I shall be unable to accept your kind invitation to tea this afternoon." Or: "My dear Mr. Browning, I must really write & thank you for all your kindness to me while I was at Cambridge . . ."

This was from an undergraduate—John Baldwyn Beversford, undergraduate 1907–12 at King's: "I write to you because I know you are always ready to give young fellows a helping hand if you can." "Thank you very much for your good criticism & advice. As soon as I can, I will write something in a purely journalist style about trains, or gardens or something nothing to do with history." Or: "I also remember well—how after one of your lectures on 1820–1830, you called me aside and asked me how it was I was never in my lodgings before twelve o'clock at night: I tremblingly replied that I spend convivial evenings with my friends, whereupon you simply said, 'You want more sleep!'" And after he leaves King's: "My dear Mr. Browning, I must really write to thank you for all your kindness to me while I was at Cambridge."

And this from a prisoner, R. Burton, 1911–12, languishing in Rochester Borstal Institution, to whom O.B. had sent a book on gardening: "Dear Sir I promis you fatful that I am gonto live a strat and honst life. Dear Sir I am pleas to hear that you will be a frend to me onc a gan I am sorey for wat I done and hope you will for give me. I am still in the gardness and all the flowers ar lovley nou I think I have sid all I can this tim so I must Bring my Letter to a cloes with my very Best lov to you so I reman yor ever Loving frend R. Burton pleas rite soon xxxxxxxx"

Fifteen.

I was standing at a window in my rooms in the college and below in the courtyard, I saw an undergraduate holding his slim-wheeled bicycle balanced by one hand, his other hand at his nape below a loose knot of blond hair, poised, as if thinking out what action he was about to take.

He stood in late sunlight slanting among the columns of the colonnade at one end of the courtyard, and he was looking down thoughtfully, his clear face shining in the sunlight.

Why can't I give myself a name?

Why, why can't I give him a name?

I don't want to define him in terms of his background, in terms of his education and knowledge, in terms of his habits and mannerisms, not even in terms of looks that made him uniquely him and no one else.

Just this: whatever his age was—and I want to think of him as ageless—I was fifteen years older, but I was not ageless.

He was very beautiful, and his beauty was why I wanted to meet him.

And how did I meet him?

I was in my rooms, dressing for the first feast of the academic year in which gowns were to be worn over dinner jackets or lounge suits for men, evening dress for women.

(Doctors were to wear scarlet.) I was in my pleated formal shirt, without trousers, trying to fit cufflinks into my cuffs, fumbling. Someone knocked on my door, and I opened, and there he was.

"Yes?" I asked, my cuffs dangling.

"I'm sorry," he said.

"Sorry? Nothing to be sorry about," I said. "Why aren't you getting ready for the feast?"

"I thought I wouldn't go."

"Of course you must go. Go to your room now and dress."

How I liked being the don telling the undergraduate what to do.

"But I haven't accepted the invitation."

"I'll get you a place."

"I honestly don't want to come."

"You'll come," I said, holding out an arm with the loose sleeve and in the other hand the cufflinks. "You can help me with these."

He hesitated.

"Come along," I said, and, dear God, I watched him, frowning a little, insert each link—gold, oval, simple—into a cuff and secure it with the little mechanism at the end with the tips of his fingers, his hands, I noted, large and masculine for such a slim young man.

"You'll now go dress for the feast," I said, as if commanding. "We'll meet tomorrow afternoon and we'll talk."

He thanked me and, turning away from him, I saw his slender nape and fine hairs from the knot loose about it.

I tied my black bowtie, drew on my trousers, and slipped the braces (I, an American, had assumed an English vocabulary in England) over my shoulders, fastened the cummerbund (English? American?), put on my jacket with black silk lapels and then my black academic gown over my dinner jacket, and went out to Hall.

I spoke to the butler who, with a slight frown, said he would find a place for the undergraduate.

Imagine candle flames in little red paper shades along the long, white cloth-covered tables, some of the shades burned about the edges; the silver; the bowls of chrysanthemums; the rows of white shirt fronts and black ties, the rows of faces along the long tables.

Behind high table, on a table draped in black velvet, the huge pieces of college silver taken from the vault, ewers, huge dishes, vases. And remember: behind the silver on the table draped, like an altar, with black velvet, was the tapestry given to the college by Morgan Forster.

Suspended above the Hall, at the far end from high table, was a gallery from where the choir sang.

I was drunk. I tried to chat up the third-year undergraduate next to me, but he didn't respond, as if he found everything too antiquated to be of any interest.

He remained sitting when "God Save the Queen" was sung by the choir from the high gallery.

I stood. An American, I had just a year or so before becoming British, and the queen was my Queen.

The undergraduate did not appear at the feast, and I looked about for an empty space where he might have been, but saw none. He never appeared at any of the college feasts.

Back in my room, very drunk, I thought: all I wanted, just that, was to undo his knot of hair and let it hang loose about his nape.

Why, I wondered, had he come to my rooms?

Sixteen.

Oh yes, I learned about the world of the undergraduates at the college. The graduates were a separate world within the world of the college. The world of the undergraduates revolved, for me, about my writing sessions.

Perhaps I was inspired to tell them what had become my own inspiration in my writing, which was to get away from description—which was not to depend on the sausages on the grill spluttering, or the sickly green water in the glass vase of dead flowers, or the dust fluffs under the bed rolling out slowly whenever the bed was made—which was to write with attention to writing as writing free of the excesses of description. I used such examples from English literature that had, in fact, been suggested to me by an historian don whose clear-edged prose I admired and who answered my asking him if he had been inspired by a writer from the past with, yes, Daniel Defoe, and I thought, I'll tell my students this. I found I talked more about the writing of past English writers than the writing put on my table and meant to be discussed—writers who had not been locked into the elaborations of descriptive writing but whose writing had music in it, such as, oh, Gibbon, such as Johnson, such as Swift, such as Newman, such as Pater—

Given the conditions I have tried to explain as constituting art;—then, if it be devoted further to the increase of men's happiness, to the redemption of the oppressed, or the enlargement of our sympathies with each other, or to such presentment of new or old truth about ourselves and our relation to the world as may ennoble and fortify us in our sojourn here, or immediately, as with Dante, to the glory of God, it will be also great art; if, over and above those qualities I summed up as mind and soul—has something of the soul of humanity in it, and finds its logical, its architectural place, in the great structure of human life.

To me, this was grand writing, and it was daring for any writers to be in any way inspired by it, not now, not in a world that had left such grandness behind. But, no, the would-be writers about my table would not have it, no, no, and I thought that trying to impress them with this would be to change them and their world entirely, because the world of this writing was not to be lived in, and the wonder, if there was wonder, was that it had ever been a world people, English people! had lived in.

In the stories submitted to me, there were lots of sputtering sausages, fluffs of dust, vases filled with rotting stems, all straining for description to make a world that was lived in. How could I dare to try to impress upon my writers that that world had gone, was no longer the world a writer tried to bring alive for readers, but was a world straining its elaborations of description to enter, but failing, because there was only description, and, to me, very very little, if any, of the soul of humanity? To some astonishment around the table, I used the prose of, oh, Virginia Woolf as an example of this prose, as in, "The sun was sinking. The hard stone of the day was cracked and light poured through its splinters. Red and gold shot through the waves, in rapid running arrows, feathered with darkness. Erratically rays of light flashed and wandered like signals from shrunken islands, or darts shot through laurel groves by shameless, laughing boys. But the waves, as they neared the shore, were robbed of light, and fell in one long concussion, like a wall falling, a wall of grey stone, unpierced by any chink of light."

To me, this was a tumble of incoherent metaphors and similes that fell apart as it tried to impress. It had no soul.

I advised my group of writers to try to write fiction as they would write a paper for a tutorial. This was like asking them to give up on fiction altogether, which, in all cases, was good advice.

It is advice I give to myself.

They appeared, though, to like to come to my rooms, where some of them stayed on after the session, and I listened to them talk, and there was rhythm in the talk: Henry was in love with Ian (Ian was reading Chinese), but Ian was in love with Roger (reading history). Roger had never had sex before with anyone, and after Ian had seduced him by walking along the Backs with him and telling him how much he loved him, Roger, rising from the bed, said, "I consider this an aberration," which Ian didn't believe because in bed Roger knew just what to do, but Roger broke off his friendship with Ian. Just when Ian felt he would never love anyone else, he met James and fell in love with James, who had never had sex with anyone. Everyone was amazed that James had never had sex with anyone before, but Ian said it was true, as he had to teach James what to do. Henry, though he kept Ian as a close friend, was fed up with him because he wouldn't go to bed with him, and, anyway, Henry was beginning to find Ian unattractive. Henry fell in love with Andrew. Henry was reading maths and Andrew law. The trouble was that Henry was pressing himself too much on Andrew, and Andrew felt he shouldn't see Henry, especially during exams. This was a relief to Henry, who in any case was very low-sexed and when he made love hardly ever came. He found the cocks of other men repellent, really: "His cock was ghastly."

Monique asked, "But why does Henry always get the most beautiful lovers? He's so skinny and not at all good-looking and doesn't even like sex."

And Paul, sitting next to her, said, "Because he's nice, that's why."

And Monique: "But aren't I nice?"

Paul: "No you're not."

Monique: "Not to you."

King's College, I had been told at high table, was private, and the police were not allowed within the gate. Why this was said to me I wasn't sure, but wondered if I was being told that I could, there, lead as private a life as I wanted within the walls that I couldn't live outside. King's College was a club, and its members were aware it was a club, and in this club, I thought, there were no judgments made, not about class or sex or race or religion, as if the air of the college gave off a sense of freedom that everyone breathed, as if in that air the sense of freedom was not only intellectual, but, oh, subtly sensual, as only the air of an old college could be, invested with generations of the mind and the body.

The Persian scholar, Mr. Peter Avery, told me that Oscar Browning was famous for saying a teacher shouldn't know more than his subject and should be bad at teaching it. He was a senior fellow and he gave the talk at college feasts, such as at the feast for a past fellow, Beaves, about whom he would say, "He had the ability to tap an undergraduate on the head and on the shoulder and on the backside all at the same time," and, "He would pay particular attention to an undergraduate whom he thought not well-endowed," and, "He called everyone younger than he was and of whatever sex, 'my boy,'" and there was loud laughter in the Hall. This senior fellow was in charge of the college silver, and after every feast he and an assistant counted the silver knives, spoons, forks, and was very upset that, after a feast, a fork went missing, very upset because the silver was college silver.

At high table, where the conversation was not meant to be deep, but light, I talked with people at King's with whom I had nothing more in common than that we were at King's College high table, and that was where we understood one another because that was where we were. I spoke with the provost, who came from time to time to high table, a philosopher who said, "We have not begun to understand Plato."

One evening, from a dinner out with friends, I came into the college and saw, standing in the rain, the undergraduate who, despite my admonishing him to come to the College Feast, had not come, and his independence made him more beautiful. He was standing still, his arms hanging a little away from his body, and he was staring ahead. His long hair was dripping with rain. At first alarmed, I stopped and asked, "Are you all right?" and he remained as he'd been, staring, I now saw, across the lawn to the chapel, its windows illuminated, and he said, simply, "Wrong. Just look."

I thought, he will remember this all the rest of his life.

I left him reluctantly thinking he was the most beautiful young man I had ever seen in my life.

Seventeen.

There was a very conservative club at King's called the Chetwynd Society, conservative and outrageous for the minutes that were read by the secretary of the society. Women were allowed to join as honorary men. One of the undergraduates who came to writing sessions in my rooms, Martin, invited me to the reading of the minutes of the previous meeting of the Chetwynd Society, and I said, Of course, of course.

Martin was secretary of the society. His room was in Bodley, and to prepare for his reading the minutes, he emptied the room of his bed and all furniture but a table. By eleven thirty, the space was packed with Chetwynd members and their guests, and Martin went about among the Chetwynd members and their guests, female and male, pouring out bitters from a metal jug into pint glasses.

At midnight there were shouts of, "Minutes! Minutes!" with stomping of feet and hitting the walls. Martin left the room to go out into the passage and returned without trousers (a tradition?) and stood on the table with the large minutes books and shouted above the roar, "Gentlemen!"

He opened the ledger.

"The minutes of the 1,267th meeting of the Chetwynd Society, held in the octagonal splendor of Mr. Richards' rooms, on Friday, the twenty-sixth of April, 1985.

"Gentlemen of the Society!

"'I need not tell you,' our beloved Lay Dean boomed out to me, 'that some of the Society's elaborate rituals—' gentlemen, whatever did he mean?—'are expressly forbidden!' What do you suppose there is to make this Society so loathed by the Lay Dean? I do wonder what the Lay Dean fantasizes are the Society's elaborate rituals, however much his imagination is known throughout the college—nay, throughout Cambridge—for its own gruesome elaborations." The secretary blushes.

"Early into the Society's meeting came Mr. Jonathan Clare, a member, who invited Mr. Patricia Graham, a nonmember, for Mr. Clare to impress Mr. Graham by the proceedings. They were heard to engage in such conversation that consisted, on the part of Mr. Graham, of: yes, she would—no, she wouldn't—ooh!—she didn't know if she wanted to—no she couldn't. Mr. Clare used gentle persuasion. Ooh, perhaps! Ever more gentle persuasion. Well, yes, she would—join the Society!

"Suddenly, there was a horrible, screaming scene when Mr. Patrick Pettworth arrived and proceeded to throw an enormous—well, let's not flatter him—sort of piqued tantrum, accusing the secretary of scandal. Fie, gentlemen, fie—the dangers of being secretary, who is above scandal, but has eyes to see, ears to hear, and blushes that there should be such low levels of moral standing among the members, so that, with the responsibility of a conscientious secretary, he reminded Mr. Patrick Pettworth that it was not for scandal that he had noted that Mr. Pettworth followed too closely behind the choir as they processed towards the chapel, but for rectitude. The secretary heard Mr. Claremont say to Mr. Pleasant, 'Oh yah, I've 'ad er,' to which Mr. Pleasant responded, 'E'en awful?' Gentlemen of the Society, do you think they were discussing a nocturnal encounter between Mr. James Stout with the hefty and gruesome Mr. Sarina Platts?" And the Secretary saw Mr. Henry Dorver leave the meeting with his guest Mr. Clarence Potts, off to a hand-in-hand walk along the Backs, perhaps to drown themselves in the Cam.

"The subscriptions have amounted to £1.73. And so closes the meeting."

I asked Martin about the undergraduate I had seen in the rain, and I had hoped might be at the meeting and he said, "Oh, him, he's everywhere and nowhere."

"Do you know him?"

"No one knows him."

Still, I wondered why he had come to my rooms.

PRIVATE

Eighteen.

He came to my rooms.

He hadn't given me a story, or any writing, to discuss, so whatever the reason was for his coming to my rooms was open, and, oh, open to what?

How to describe the sense that comes with being with someone beautiful, really the only reason for being with him, the sense of, oh, promise, but only the sense of promise, a sense that held me as within a spirit of, yes, joy.

And there was some joy in him as a person, for he revealed that he took pleasure bantering with me, lightly—"bantering," as I learned, an old Etonian word that he had picked up at Eton. He was one of the few Etonians to come to King's, which had in the past been the college for that school to transfer to. Past, now past. King's had now become plebian, except, perhaps, for him, or so I liked to think of him, from a past that, except for him, had gone.

I asked him what he was reading.

He was reading Classics.

He had read Classics at Eton, where he had been known as a Rho Kappa.

Bantering, he asked, "What does ancient Greece mean to you?" And as we were sitting side-by-side on the sofa, he put a hand on my shoulder, so I was suddenly embarrassed by the intimacy and drew away.

And he seemed to react against his own gesture of intimacy. for he stood up from the sofa and sat in an armchair.

He said he was fed up with his Greek studies.

Fed up?

Yes, he was fed up. All he had learned of the Greek Classics was the old received English vision of ancient Greece.

"That vision inspired E.M. Forster," I said.

"The fantasy is all in E.M. Forster."

That was all he had to say about E.M. Forster?

That was all.

Yet, I felt that he was not condemning Forster, but me, and I tried to temper my resentment, more for the sake of E.M. Forster than for myself.

He went on, and I felt, more, that he was trying to contend with me. He derided, he said, the fantasies of sex about classical Greece. The fantasies aroused by the *Symposium*. So much confused talk about the *erastês* and the *erômenos* and *erôs*, the lover and the beloved and erotic love itself—so much confused talk about sexual relations between a lover and a beloved and love, leading finally to what? To a man inserting his erection between the legs of a boy and ejaculating, the cum dripping down the boy's legs which he wipes away with a rag? That is meant to be what virtue leads to? After, do they both feel they have become better citizens, wiser, more courageous, the beloved ready himself to become a lover? All because of an act that is never described in the *Symposium*, so that if we had only the *Symposium* to rely on, we'd think that sex was enacted in ways that boggle attempts at the most elaborate fantasies. We know what the sex was by drawings on drinking vases, intercrural sex, not, it appears, very elaborate, not a great fulfillment of virtue, whatever virtue was. Fantasies, fantasies!

The fact was that I was enjoying his rant, because I believed it did have to do with his talking about himself.

To keep him going, I asked him if he ever fantasized about beautiful Alcibiades, come to the Symposium drunk, his crown of flowers askew on is head, intent on sharing the couch with Socrates, the envy of all?

Alcibiades was an egomaniac, an exploiter of the famous, an ignominious political opportunist, a fraud, a traitor.

I clapped my hands and said, "Oh, good, very good."

I was being false. I wanted him to think that I appreciated his attack on the fantasy of a Greece that had never existed but in the mind of E.M. Forster, as if the attack on Forster, on all the fantasies of Greece, was meant to be an attack on me for all the fantasy he had to have intuited in me. But, yes, I was being false, and I was sure he knew that I was being false. And I was sure that he, too, was being false, and knew that his attack on Greece was an attempt to expose in me all the feelings I had for him, which I thought he had begun to mock. Well, he did, I think, recognize those feelings, however mockingly. And I had to clap at his mocking me, as if he were mocking all of ancient Greece.

I thought, I'm not sure I like him.

I didn't want him to feel that I was paying the special attention to him that I did pay, so I followed the fluttering flight of a large moth about the room.

He saw that I was concentrating on the moth, and he rose from his chair and picked up a magazine, and rolled it and went after the moth, which he smashed with the rolled-up magazine when it settled on a windowpane.

"Why did you do that?" I asked.

He said, "Because you were more attentive to it than to me."

Startled, I laughed an awkward laugh. I said, "You have my attention."

He laughed what I could only imagine was a knowing laugh wicked in its knowingness—knowingness about me, whatever he did know about me.

He put his cup of tea on the table by him.

I didn't want him to leave, and though there seemed to be no reason for him to stay, I felt that he wanted to stay. As he was rising from his armchair, I offered him more tea, now with biscuits, and he sat back and said, yes, that would be lovely.

The chapel bell rang. Had I been to Evensong? No, not yet, though I'd been wanting to attend. He abruptly told me to put on my gown and we'd go, and I did, and I followed him. The chapel windows were lit. The service had begun. We sat at the very back of the chapel, on stone ledges, facing the great wooden reredos, through the great gateway of which I saw the carved ends of the pews, saw white surplices and glowing candles, everything partly dissolved in the bright, warm light, and I looked up over the screen to the fan vaulting where the voices of the choir rose and themselves fanned out in delicate reverberation. I seemed to be sitting a long, long way back from the chapel itself, seemed to be viewing down long, long perspective lines, seemed to be viewing from darkness into light, seemed to hear from silence the voices.

He left me and I returned to my seat, wondering where he had gone off to. After every time he left me, I wondered where he had gone off to.

I wondered: What was that all about? Well, what?

But he came back often, knocking on my door. Yes, tea was ordered from the pantry, with, yes, rounds of smoked salmon, cress, cucumber sandwiches, the butter thick.

The sunlight through a window brightened a Turkey rug.

And, yes, yes, we were contained and safe in this temporary world, in which everything seemed at least temporarily possible, whatever might be possible.

And he, on the sofa, a little languidly at ease in this undefined sense of possibility.

I sat in an armchair.

He told me bits that he had discovered in his reading about the Classics that amused him. Ione of Chios knew of a letter beyond the alphabet, a letter that had no written sign, a letter used by Greeks and Latins, pronounced *aggulus*. What letter in what words this was used for is forgotten.

Oh, and how could I not note the sleeves of his loose white shirt rolled up tightly to his elbows, the collar open? I thought, again, the English ideal, belied by casualness, by not really caring if the tea was tepid, the rounds of sandwiches a little stale, that the rug was dusty, not caring that his shirt was wrinkled, the collar threadbare.

Sustain this, sustain this.

I was in England, England existed, here, now, in Cambridge, at least for moments. It must not be made emphatic—it must not be commented on—it must even be deflected from itself by incidentals, but it was here, or the idea of it was.

The idea was manifested in the teapot and cups (a metal teapot, the cups squat and thick, but with the King's coat of arms on each, in books scattered on the Turkey rug (dog-eared paperback books bought from a stall in Market Square), and something more, something more.

He was my delight. I didn't love him, no, didn't dare love him, but he was my delight.

Oh, the potency of an idea!

Twenty.

An aside—

Now, please, allow me to go on about the long past of English teatime, or, better, the American idea of an English tea, preferably out on a lawn sloping down from a large house with a pillared porch climbed up to by a flight of worn stone steps, the table by a smoothly flowing river below the house and the green lawn, the table set with Chinese porcelain cups and a silver teapot, the accoutrements needed to realize the fantasy. And so, I can visualize the idea, for I'd read about such teatimes, and the idea is visualized in the setting of the long shadows of the summer sun of the company cast moving about, and the delicate accoutrements. But if, after years, I myself still have received ideas about such a ceremony, I recall the conversation among those gathered for the ceremony—what can I say, an American in his first year of half a century of years of living in England and assuming what he at first believed was the eternal ceremony of English tea, with an emphasis on the *eternal*? I recall the conversation was at best banal, far inferior to the cups and teapot and the cake stand with a fruitcake, which, themselves, evoked the eternal meaning of teatime.

During my many years in London, teatime became reduced to mugs at a table in the kitchen, the conversation, however, more and more original, for I found that the British themselves had no firm idea of what it was to be British, which questioning I at least found interesting, as if the British were looking through their own received ideas of what was meant by their being British; they more and more to referred themselves, as I found among my friends, not so much to being British, but as from Yorkshire or Wales or Scotland or, best of all, London. I associated with this because I had no idea in what way I was American, because I didn't see myself as American, but as someone born and brought up in a French speaking parish, as though born and brought up within a palisade of trees from a vast dark forest.

And I insert here a poem I wrote in French that infers everything that there is to know about that past.

Il y a longtemps que je n'ai pas prier,
Mais pendant la nuit
Je me suis perdu dans la fôret
Et j'entends une voix
Qui vient de loin, dire,
Dieu, Dieu, ayez pitié de nous,
Et encore plus loin de cette voix
J'entends le bruit des hâches dans la fôret.

I had no firm idea of what world the undergraduate referred himself to—he never did say much about his world—so my idea of his world was one with his high-caste beauty, but if he was, to me, of a high caste he was of a caste that had inherited grand silver but could not afford to hire a servant to polish it. I imagined him in a world in which he carried tea things on a tray to his mother, by way of a doorway that was a false shelf of the backs of books, into the corner of a library where his mother sat in an armchair, her feet on a footstool, a rug over her lap, and her dogs lying about her, and there would be talk about how to continue to live in such a house. But, no, not really. There was nothing I could truly imagine about his world because I didn't know it, and even if I had been to houses in the country where I might have thought he fit in and where I then put him in, I would have got it all wrong. I presumed on what I didn't know. I presumed, for example, the caste he belonged to was passing, had passed, though he could easily have belonged to a caste that was in fact very much present, and I had no idea what that was, except that it was more truly itself, as being Welsh or Scots or from Yorkshire or London was being more truly oneself than being British. Well, I didn't know where he fit in.

Twenty-one.

Set this next scene, a hazy Saturday afternoon, where? Does it matter if it is set in a public house in Granchester, if you don't know what pub or where Granchester is? And the scene seen or heard? Try: heard. But not heard, not in here, unless the words sound in the mind. But try. So: voices of people in the pub, voices near and distant, and from the hubbub words, "as I was saying," and "I said," and "listen, love," and "you said," and "you are a dear," that rise and fall, fall and rise, and our voices among them. And a beat from somewhere in the midst, a constant beat at a low and sometimes high vibration, as if all hearts were synchronized and all voices were set to that beat, high and low.

And for those readers who want to see, this will do: hollyhocks in the garden of the public house, seen through a many-paned window, bicycles leaning against a garden shed? Or this: the garden autumn wilted, dripping with rain, and wet umbrellas hung on the backs of chairs and dripping puddles on the bare wooden floor? Or snow falling outside and a small fire on the grate, the flickering flames reflected in the wainscoting?

Ha, how I want to write, not for what is seen, but what is heard!

After a long silence during which I wondered what he was thinking, he suddenly said he was trying to hum a tune, which was there, there in his mind, but he couldn't hum it.

"Try," I asked.

He shook his head.

He tried to hum the tune, but couldn't, and he said, "Oh give up, give up."

I asked him not to give up.

He lowered his head, and I saw a blush rise from his cheeks to his forehead. When he looked up at me, he tried, for me, to hum the tune, but he couldn't, he couldn't.

"I'm sorry," he said.

He was as if unconscious of himself, but I was altogether conscious of him, the top buttons of his white shirt open and he touching, with his index finger, his chest.

I sensed his thinking go round, then stop, and he suddenly asked, "What do you want from me?"

He couldn't have said anything that would have made me more attentive, and I suspected that he wanted my attention for him to test me with it. Well, I would let him test me with his attention.

"What do you mean, what do I want from you?" I asked.

"Oh—"

Again, his thinking appeared to go round and round, as he, often blinking, considered the thoughts as they went round. I watched him, and when he looked at me steadily his thinking stopped on me.

I waited.

I couldn't bear to look at him, and I felt that I was being drawn far, far out, so far out on a lake or a body of water that he appeared to me in miniature, surrounded by dark. And he became more beautiful to me than ever, there, now surrounded by dark, and, as if fixed by portraiture, the long finger of his large hand poised in the gesture of touching his chest exposed by the opening in his loose white shirt.

Explain to him why what he had said had such an effect on me that all I could do was stare at him? What did I want from him? I wouldn't make myself vulnerable to him, but he sensed something about me, or had heard something about me, that he knew would make me stand and look down at him, he looking up at me with a tight smile. What, I thought, did he know about my life—what I didn't want him to know but that, at the same time, what I did want him to know, the strange sense of keeping my dark secrets and wanting those secrets to be revealed in harsh bright light by another? Enough of this. I stood and placed pound notes on the table.

"Will I see you again?" he asked, and I wondered why he might think he wouldn't see me again.

I said, "I'll see you sometime in my set," and, to suggest at least some promise in our relationship that had almost ended just then, I added, "Try to hum the tune going round your head."

He said, "I'll try."

Outside, I stood still for a long moment, then the thought came to me: it was not that he thought I wanted something from him, I didn't want anything from him but to be with him, because he had in a quizzical way become my student, though he had his own tutor and his own revisions and papers to write.

The question was what did he want from me?

I went back into the pub, but stopped within when I saw him, still at the table where I had left him, alone in the midst of others, he, his eyes closed, as if concentrating on the tune that was going round in his head, and I left.

I am sorry that I can't seem to create in him a distinct personality, but perhaps I didn't want him to have a distinct personality. He was my fantasy, and though the fantasy was embodied in him, he appeared to have, beneath his loose clothes, a fantasy body. I knew I was in love with a fantasy.

Twenty-two.

How often I've wondered: we listen to music on the most spiritual level, we look at paintings on the most spiritual level, we read poems on the most spiritual level, all without believing in the spirit that hovers at that level, so what is it that we do not believe in that moves us and raises us to that level?

I told myself, once again, that I didn't want to know about his past, wanted to know only about his present presence.

He was by upbringing, of course, civil, and would have known how to engage with others invited to a weekend in the country, or so I imagined. However, at King's he was not social, or at least he never brought any friends to my rooms, nor mentioned any. I would not have been jealous of his friends, but his self-containment as a loner did make me jealous, as if as a loner he could leave me at any moment.

He could have let go of me at any moment, and in fact would sometimes suddenly leave me, not saying goodbye, and yet when I next saw him, I felt he had come because he wanted to be with me.

I am going to use a literary device, which is to use the past continuous tense to describe an event that occurred in the simple past, because the event resounds in my memory in the past continuous.

We'd take walks, and on the walks along the Backs he, both arms raised high, would holler at punters on the Cam, and I would see in him a sudden spontaneity toward the world at large that was unexpected, for he always appeared disengaged from the world, but now would appear engaged, engaged with exchanging hollered hellos with punters he wouldn't have known, and laughing when one of the young men in the punt would stand and shake a bottle of champagne and aim it at the bank so the cork would fly out and, yes, hit him in the middle of the chest. He would then fall to the ground and pretend to have been killed. I would help him up.

And let me note this about the way he would dress: brogues, white and tan, and trousers a little too big for him but cinched in with a belt tightly at the waist, his wrinkled white shirt tucked in, and, if wearing a jumper, a white jumper with a V neckline with fine red and blue stripes along the V. Well, typical for the times, or perhaps an even earlier time, because I know I impose images from the great store of images of England that fill my head, whether or not the images apply, because, though I have lived here for such a long time, I don't really know London, or England, or, much less, Great Britain, but I don't think anyone does. It would only be a fraudulent nostalgia that would make me use the continuous past in writing about the past, though I suppose I do accuse myself of that fraudulent nostalgia, and we know that nostalgia has nothing to do with history.

But we would go to recitals together, and, after, walking together along deserted—yes, yes, moonlit—streets of Cambridge.

Now to revert to the simple past.

High on the music as I expected him to be, I said, "That was so moving."

"Moving?" he suddenly asked.

"You weren't moved?"

He said that the pianist had lost his way, and had had to get back into the score open before him on the piano, and, no, he wasn't moved.

I was impressed, as I certainly had not noted the pianist losing his way in the performance, and this young man had.

I said, "You know more about music than I do."

"Do I?"

"I believe that you do, and that you are more enchanted by music than I am."

He asked, "What do you mean by enchantment?"

"Don't you know?"

"I'm not sentimental."

"And you think I am?"

"I suspect you are very sentimental."

"I am?"

"I think you are."

He had never before made a comment to me about myself, and this meant he thought about me when he was alone.

I stopped walking and he did, standing facing me. I said, "I dare say you're right," and I continued, "is that wrong of me?

"No, no," he said quietly.

I had never before thought I was in any way sentimental, and yet he had warned me about something so personal it couldn't be about me, but about himself.

He suddenly said, "I have to understand my sentiments."

"Understand?"

He said he had to understand himself, had to understand his feelings before he expressed them, before he acted on them. He was not sentimental, as he believed I was, but he did have feelings, he had such feelings he didn't understand, but he had to understand them.

Was he fearful of them?

Perhaps, he said.

Did he talk to anyone about them?

He did, to the chaplain.

To the chaplain?

Yes.

I told him he could talk to me, because I wanted to know him, wanted even to help him, if he thought I could in any way help him.

He repeated, he talked to the chaplain.

He understands?

Yes, he does.

And I wouldn't?

He looked away.

I said I wondered why he saw me, I wondered, in fact, why *I* wanted to see him, the only undergraduate I had become close to. Did he think I was sentimental about our friendship?

Again, he looked past me, or through me, at that vast distance , so far I imagine he was looking into the universe.

I saw in his face as I stared at him an intelligent beauty.

Desire came over me with a movement in me, though all I could think was that the desire was for something he would have considered sentimental, for I was now characterized by him as sentimental just by that one poetic comment about music, and it was up to me to show him I was not.

I said, Go to your room now.

Desire was to me a state in itself, and it was mostly a playful state, but which demanded fulfilment.

Sustain the desire in itself, I thought, and never try to fulfill it.

But desire longs for fulfillment.

Twenty-three.

He appeared to be a constant presence in my set—*appeared*, because he was mostly in his room working on revisions and papers for his tutorials, and I in my set had submissions of writing to consider for the sessions, and also, as the autumn so slowly deepened into dark skies, to work on a novel, one set in London.

What I remember now is his seeming to spend long teatimes in my sitting room, much of that time he reading and I reading, the teacups empty, the teapot cold, and one sandwich left on the King's College dish with the college's coat of arms, three roses, gules charged on the dexter side with a fleur-de-lis and on the sinister with a lion passant guardant, printed in royal purple on the rim of the dish, and the sense about us was that we were members of a club that no one from the outside world had any right to question, because we were within King's College, where, of course, dons had undergraduates to their rooms for tutorials and teas and, too, sherry, and if there were laws, they were too old, from 1441 when the college was founded by Henry VI, to be questioned, even by the Kingsmen.

While he, in an armchair, read, I, at my desk, worked on my novel, which I knew was too abstract, though I so wanted to write a novel in which ideas, ideas hardly manifested in objects, would call for the reader's attention. I did think that novels had become—and why and from when would be the subject of a study I took notes for—too dependent on cups of tea and teapot and dishes of sandwiches and rugs and armchairs and sofas and tables and chairs, and I strained my writing to rise higher, to where the novel would be condemned for what it so strained to do, that is, to rise to the level of the immortal soul, which would be condemned by critics because there was, there is, no immortal soul, but there was, there are, only teacups and teapots and dishes of sandwiches. And this is the world we live in.

I wanted, oh, clarity, even, if possible, a clarity intelligible in itself, with nothing in the clarity to obscure it.

The sitting room appeared to be filled with daylight that changed according to clouds passing, so the light faded into dimness and then, suddenly, was bright. I, at my desk writing, would poise my pen over the page and look at him, as if he was revealed in that sudden brightness reading, I supposed, about Homeric meter. His large, bare feet were propped on the coffee table among piles of books, and there were piles of books on the floor, and from time to time he picked up one randomly and read, as if his reading on Homeric meter was as random as any of his reading. That was it: a seeming randomness in him of attention, but once he was attentive, he was fully so, his eyes focused and the space between his eyebrows furrowed with the doubt that what was printed on the page could possibly be true, even if reading about Homeric meter. I liked this doubt in him—that anything could be true, an indication, to me, of his superiority, because of course the superior always doubted everything, though they did keep their doubts to themselves, expressed only by a slight tension between the brows. I liked it when he looked at me with those focused eyes and that furrow between his eyebrows, doubting everything I said.

You may think it didn't happen, that it is but an affectation in my writing. After hours of autumn dimness and lamps lit, a sudden brightness came into the room when I heard him say, "Ankle deep in flowers," and I looked up from my writing and saw him holding out a book that he appeared, not to be reading, but staring through.

"What's that?" I asked.

"You don't know?"

"I don't."

"I'll give you some hints," he said, and he turned pages and read out: "And like a finer light in light . . ." But I had to admit I still couldn't guess. He read, "And every thought breaks out a rose."

I put down my pen, as if that was a distraction, and I said, "That is wonderful."

"You think so?"

"Isn't it to you?"

He closed the book and let it drop to his lap. "Not as much as it is to you." He smiled, his smile twisting only one side of his lips. "You find too much too wonderful."

"Do I?"

"Don't you know you do?"

"No one before you has told me so."

"Well, I'm telling you."

I nodded, in a way accepting his saying this. Again, any attention he had towards me I not only accepted, I wanted. And I made myself more vulnerable to him by ignorantly asking, again, who wrote those lines.

He said he'd give me another hint and picked up the book from his lap and read, as if from anywhere, "But there is more than I can see, and what I see I leave unsaid, nor speak it . . ."

"I'm sorry," I said, "that's not enough for me to recognize the work."

He closed the book against my ignorance.

"You won't tell me?"

He said, "No, I won't."

"I am sorry," I said, and I saw in his pleading eyes that he wanted me to react to the poetry. "Please go on and quote."

"Another time."

"I really am sorry."

"Then, I will, I will for you," he said, and he read.

"Dark house, by which once more I stand
Here in the long unlovely street,
Doors, where my heart was used to beat
So quickly, waiting for a hand,

"A hand that can be clasp'd no more—
Behold me, for I cannot sleep,
And like a guilty thing I creep
At earliest morning to the door.

"He is not here; but far away
The noise of life begins again,
And ghastly thro' the drizzling rain
On the bald street breaks the blank day."

He rested his head on the back of the armchair, and he raised his arms and crossed them over his head in a sudden gesture of what I thought anguish.

And if it was possible to have a sense of someone's soul, if it possible for the latency of the soul to become the sense that his soul was in anguish, I had it, I had that sense. And for the first time, I became anxious having him come so often to my set, because the sense roused in me was that there was nothing I could do for him. He was a loner. I didn't love him.

I waited until he lowered his arms and I saw he looked past me, and I thought he was looking into a vast distance.

"I'm sorry," he said.

"Don't be sorry," I said.

You may not believe this, but the room darkened with a dark cloud. He said, "It doesn't matter."

"Oh, it matters."

"Does it?"

"Yes, it does."

"What does it matter?"

And I, with a lilt, said, "Something."

He again crossed his arms over his head and lay back for a long while, and I left him to go out and down to the combination room, because I was frightened. On my return, he had gone.

Twenty-four.

There lived at King's someone who was known as the last of Bloomsbury, almost an invisible presence because he was mostly hidden away in his rooms. He was an old don named George—or, as he was known by everyone, Dadie—Rylands. He had come from Eton to King's in 1920, when he'd read Classics with Sheppard; he, a beautiful young man and a homosexual, had been taken up by the older homosexual Maynard Keynes, who introduced him to Lytton Strachey and Leonard and Virginia Woolf, for whom he worked at the Hogarth Press. He had known Thomas Hardy in Hardy's last years.

It was arranged for me to meet him in his rooms in the Old Lodge for drinks. Outside the windows a view of deep green lawn, the Cam and its bridges to the left, the Gibbs Building to the right, and beyond the Gibbs the façade of the chapel, and in the room, covering all surfaces, silver plates and candlesticks and tankards and painted china teapots, cups and saucers, bowls, all Dadie's collection. There were two other Fellows, all of us, Dadie said, to form a *petit cercle* about him. He moved and talked rapidly and constantly, saying, I wasn't quite sure about anyone or everyone. "So lively, so gay, so life-enhancing." I wondered if there was anyone he had ever known who was not lively, gay, life-enhancing, and if there wasn't something mocking in his tone.

(I was told later that he spoke with what was called "the Eton banter.")

On a seat in the bow windows, Virginia Woolf had thought of writing *A Room of One's Own*, in which she described the luncheon she'd been invited to with E.M. Forster and Maynard Keynes, now married to the Russian ballet dancer Lydia Lopokova.

Here is a passage:

"The wineglasses had flushed yellow and flushed crimson; had been emptied; had been filled . . . No need to hurry. No need to sparkle. No need to be anyone but oneself . . . how admirable friendship and the society of one's kind, as lighting a good cigarette, one sunk among the cushions in the window seat."

Dadie took out bottles from a corner cupboard whose doors, as all the doors and the fireplace, had been decorated by Dora Carrington, who was so hopelessly in love with the homosexual Lytton Strachey, and we all drank our drinks as quickly as Dadie did. It was time to go to the Senior Combination Room, and someone helped him on with his gown.

On our way, keeping everyone close about himself as if for protection, he talked rapidly about having been at Eton, when most Eton boys came to King's, and where Aldous Huxley taught him. Huxley, almost blind, had to hold the book he was reading from out loud close to one eye, so he couldn't see beyond the book. If he asked for a book, the students would get from the library the biggest book they could find, and, behind it, Huxley couldn't possibly see them, and they'd sneak out.

In the crowded Senior Combination Room, he gathered his *petit cercle* ever closely about himself, saying, "Don't leave me. Don't leave me." And when the butler announced dinner, he asked us to gather still more closely about him, his arms locked, it seemed, in all of ours, so that when we got to the table, we'd all be able to sit together. "I don't want to lose you," he said. He hadn't been to high table in over a year. We all managed to sit together at the end of the table. He said, "I don't come. You may find you don't know the Fellow who sits next you. And George, the butler, is retiring. Even more reason for not coming. And have you heard the college carpenter is retiring?"

We walked him back to the Old Lodge. He said, "When I was an undergraduate, the whole making of my life was in interaction with the dons, and I hope that, at least for the first twenty years that I was a Fellow, I helped in the making of the lives of some undergraduates. I do hope."

When I learned that Dadie Rylands had died, I went to see my friend the scholar of Persian literature, Mr. Peter Avery. He apologized that he couldn't be immediately attentive to me; a gentleman was there, winding an antique clock. After the clock winder left, he asked me into his study, the bookshelves packed with Persian books, and with a window out on the lawn of the Backs and the Cam, and Peter Avery smoking cigarette after cigarette, he talked about Dadie.

When Dadie was too weak to get out of bed, my friend visited him, sat on his bed, and held his hand, and Dadie said, "But they're all mad. And there is nothing one can do." His collection of silver and china were taken by his family, but, along with the children's books, he did give to the college six eighteenth-century—1725 or thereabouts—salvers of silver.

Peter said, "You'll see how sad his rooms are now," and came with me to see them. The long passage with bookcases on either side that I recalled packed with books were now half empty, with cardboard cartons of books on the floor. The large North Room was empty of furniture, and the bow windows looking out onto the Great Lawn was without its sofa. The four doors and fireplace surround painted by Carrington were still in place, but only a few china plates were left, emphasizing the absence of all the silver, cups and saucers, bibelots. Paintings hung askew on the walls, and on the floor, propped against the wall, was a brownish-yellowish painting of Lytton Strachey, who had been in love with Dadie, overlapped by a bright, overly Impressionist-like painting of hydrangeas. In the now empty bathroom, Rylands shortly before he died had collapsed in the bath and called out for eight hours before he was discovered. The South Room had some furniture pushed anyhow, and in the bedroom was a big stain on the wallpaper where the bed had been. There was a sense of underlying tattiness, with a smell of impacted dust.

Twenty-five.

I apologized, but I had to go to high table, as I had signed in. The undergraduate looked about my sitting room, as if for something he had left behind. Hesitantly, he asked if he could stay in my set while I was at high table. He had eaten. If he wanted to stay in my rooms, I said, of course, if he wanted. At high table, I thought of my lover, as I had begun to consider him because he had put that idea into my head but ever again referred to it, as if it had left him, and it occurred to me that he was always, in his way, bantering. He was in my rooms, and I wondered what he was doing there.

Back there, I found, in the sitting room, his books and his shoes, but not him. Frowning, I went into my bedroom and saw him asleep on my bed, the bedside lamp lit, he face up so the light shone on his forehead, cheeks, chin, lips. I had the momentary shock that he was not breathing, and I approached the bed to lean over him to see that his chest rose and fell lightly. And I sat on a chair by the bed and looked at him. I will not try to account for the feelings that came over me, that rose and fell in me, over and over, as I silently stared at him lying on my bed, his breathing so light he might not have been breathing.

Help me, dear God, in this.

I didn't want him to wake up, no, not then, I wanted to sit and stare at him asleep. But that was morbid, and I reached out and shook his shoulder. He opened his eyes slowly, and appeared surprised to see me, then quickly sat up and apologized, he'd felt so very sleepy, suddenly, that he'd thought of nothing more than a short nap, and came into my bedroom. But he didn't get up from the bed. He looked at me as if for a reaction, positive or negative, to his having presumed to sleep on my bed. He appeared to me totally vulnerable, if not to me, to vulnerability itself, as if vulnerability could be a possession, and he had had to give in to it.

"Would you like to sleep more?" I asked tentatively, as if that were a possibility he himself considered.

He looked at me not sure who I was, then, recognizing who I was, he again sat and turned his legs over the side of the bed and stood.

"I'll go," he said.

"You can stay."

"I'll go."

And I followed him into the sitting room, where he gathered his books.

A knock on my door. An undergraduate had come to see me, but, holding the door hardly open, I made excuses, and she left. I closed the door, and I found him, sitting in an armchair, reading, the book held close to his smiling face.

How easily he could shift into outward brightness, leaving me to ask if the inner darkness I sensed in him was all in my own sense of him.

In a tone of high levity, he said, "Listen to this."

"I'm listening."

He recited, "You wonder when my fancies play/ To find me gay among the gay,"* and he smiled and slammed the book shut and laughed.

"I suppose I do," I said.

"Keep wondering."

As though suddenly cheeky, intending himself to be cheeky, he asked if he could, after all, stay for a cup of evening tea before going to his room, and I responded only if he would keep me amused, which he did, his levity almost at moments pitched high, he sounding at those moments like a pubescent boy whose voice was changing. We didn't have tea. I opened a bottle of wine from the college cellar. He became silly and taunted me with stories of dirty old men who had made passes at him, often on the underground, or in pubs, and once in the Fitzwilliam Museum. I listened, I tried to laugh; there was nothing agonizing in his talk, for his silliness disallowed any agony, any expression of agony at all.

Again, how easily he could switch from one person into another as though by a simple change of register.

I said, "Oh, do stop."

"I'm no longer amusing you?"

"I've stopped caring."

"Should I go?'

"Yes."

---

* From *In Memoriam* by Alfred Lord Tennyson.

He did not appear offended, but, instead, seemed amused by my telling him to go. Laughing, he rose and I rose and he came to me and hugged me, this time closely, and long enough for me to put my arms about him and hug him.

"I'll stay," he said.

We listened to music.

Twenty-six.

Strange, strange the awareness two people have of each other, sitting together, in subtle bodily contact with each other, listening to music, the speechless music lowering on speech its spell so we could not talk.

Heraclites said, "The unheard harmony is more powerful than the heard."

All I could allow myself was to comment on how the fugue developed. This annoyed him, not only because he knew the work better than I did, though he wouldn't say so and granted me the better knowledge, but also because he resented my pressing on him, over and over, "Listen, listen, listen to that!" and raising my hand as if to stop the music at those passages I so wanted him to be attentive to and, himself, comment upon. But he wouldn't have it, and became silent.

Too much? Too much? What was that too much? If I asked myself, it is too much, I can't bear it, what, I asked myself, was that too much?

What was that too much when, listening to music— one's attention enthralled by those moments when a trill underscores a single repeated note, that single note more and more dominant as the trill disappears and the dominant note takes over as the theme of the sonata, the theme more and more dominant, and then, suddenly, the trill emerges delicately and the theme is held back, held back again with a single note but repeated so slowly the theme sounds as if suspended in silence while the trill sustains the sound around the silence, and then, again suddenly but with a greater force, the theme breaks through the silence—what is the too much that makes one think, I can't bear this?

And one has to let go.

How to describe the "need" in someone who denies any evidence of "need"? Did I note in him a double impulse in the way he, standing before me, swayed backwards and forwards again and again, as if with the impulses to step forward toward me and step back from me, simultaneously?

I said, "It's raining."

We went to the window, on the outside of which rain was falling as though the deepening dark itself condensed into large drops that hit the pane.

Then one of those moments . . . One of those moments that has a long history but that is ahistorical, that is personal but that rises high above the daily personal into the high bright impersonal, each of us leaning against the casements on either side of the window, we were silent, and rain fell outside.

And when I said, simply, the word *rain*, the word was resonant with more than the meaning of the word, and when he repeated, as if in another register, "rain," I knew he meant more than the word. And the sound of the rain on the window, that too, had meaning. The delicate tension between us, with its low, low reverberating twangs, as of a violinist testing the strings, then playing to a chord, a long, long, rising chord, the violinist joined by other string instruments of different sonority, and the chords rising into the melodious, and the melodious into the most meaningful celestial harmony.

Did he hear?

He heard something, and he was very attentive to that something, more attentive to that something than to me.

To get close to that something, I thought, he leaned his forehead against the windowpane, on the other side of which the rain fell and dripped down.

He heard something, he heard something.

I asked, "Are you listening to the rain?"

He turned to me and smiled. He asked, "The rain?"

"Aren't you listening to the rain?"

"No."

"What, then?"

He said, "To music."

And he pressed his forehead to my chest.

Twenty-seven.

I met the chaplain crossing the lawn, which only members of the college were allowed to cross.

To integrate him more into the college, which he thought he needed, the chaplain told me he had made my, yes, my undergraduate companion a member of the Thursday Club, a dining club, the big event of which was a dinner party in a private room in a restaurant in Ely.

Oh?

Hadn't I been invited?

No.

Well, he would make sure I was.

It didn't matter, I said, though, oh, I felt it mattered more than anything else mattered.

Of course it mattered.

Instead of going on to where I had planned to go, I returned to my rooms and lay on my bed, as if waiting for the chaplain to knock on my door to say that I was invited, and it occurred to me that I would have been offended not being invited to the dining club.

Ten of us met at the Cambridge train station in the bright evening, three women and the rest men, the women in black evening gowns, the men in black tie (Joseph in his formal clerical garb). My undergraduate was at ease among the others, some of whom I was meeting for the first time, and whom he introduced me to. How to describe the lightness of spirit among us, as light as the air, as we waited on the platform for the train to Ely? How to describe the intimacy of a club of mostly young people, dressed formally in an informal setting, aware that they formed a club that was more special for being out in the public, defined now by black evening gowns and black ties? In the English manner, the evening gowns were not elegant, the suits with stained lapels, and the bowties crooked. Nor was there any indication that the undergraduates were all privileged for being rich; they were all privileged for being in the Thursday Club, and within the greater club of King's. It was as if there on the platform everyone danced about one another, the music to the dance their spirited talk and laughter. And my undergraduate among them.

I sat with the chaplain on the small rattling train. Only our party were in the carriage, the windows open to the countryside we passed, the light slanting through dark trees.

The chaplain said, "He came to me the other day to talk, and without betraying what he said I can say he suddenly began to weep, in agony."

This alarmed me.

"Will he be all right?" I asked.

He said, "He'll be if he takes care."

"Takes care of what?"

The chaplain didn't answer.

We listened to the talk and laughter of the undergraduates, and, again, I thought that it was all the chaplain's doing that my student was among them, had gone to him, and he had been helped by the chaplain.

From the Ely train station, our party—shifting about, the undergraduates' talk witty, quick, intelligent, I simply listening to it, listening, too, to my undergraduate participate in it—walked in the continuing bright evening to a restaurant near the cathedral, Norman, AD 1090.

The private room above the restaurant, The Old Fire Engine House, was prepared for us. One of the undergraduate women, Susan, put me at the head of the table and my undergraduate at the bottom, or, perhaps, he was at the head and I was at the bottom.

The Menu:

***

Tomato and Onion Soup
Smoked Mackerel

***

Chicken with Cream and Fresh Herbs
Casserole of Pigeon

***

Choice of Desserts

***

English Cheeses

***

Coffee

And many bottles of house wine—red, of no particular vintage.

I looked at my undergraduate looking at me from the far end of the now rumpled tablecloth with dishes and knives and forks and bottles of wine and wine glasses and rumpled napkins scattered. He pulled the band that kept his long hair in a knot at his nape, so his hair fell loose, and, oh, did he look down the table at me?

Then the walk through the now-deserted town of Ely, the streetlamps casting a level of yellowish light below the high level of the sky's faintly silver light, and the strange feeling of walking along the deserted streets. And the wait at the train station at Ely, no one else but our party there, even the ticket office closed. And the illuminated train arriving, and that, too, empty but for us on our way back to Cambridge.

He walked beside me from the Cambridge train station. He said he thought I'd be pleased by his telling that he was able to hum the tune that had for so long been going around in his head, and I felt a movement in me when he said, "I'll hum it to you."

I felt he might come to my rooms, and when, at night and asleep I was woken by what I thought was someone knocking at the door to my set, I got up and, naked, went to open just enough to see the dimly lit passage was empty.

In the morning the chaplain came to tell me that the beautiful young man had been found by a jogger along the Cam, drowned.

Twenty-eight.

During Lent, I often went, wearing the academic gown which allowed me to sit in the carved stalls in the chapel, to Evensong, where the only other attendant was the Divine. The service was held by the chaplain, the dean, the choirmaster, and the choir singing plainchant. From somewhere, sudden winds would make the candles, lit in glass holders, waver.

The term came to an end. During winter vac, I went to Switzerland to ski.

During the spring term, I tried to devote myself to my writing, though I did more wondering about writing than writing.

I wondered, as always: What was the appreciation of belief in a work of art if one no longer believed? What was it that moved the soul in the words, sweet soul, for the words did move in my soul?

The poet, bereaved, believed in his great love—My spirit loved and loves him yet—and so mustn't the reader believe in love? How to read the friend of mine who lives in God* with what impact, unless one believed in God? Belief must, somehow, be expressed in what was written, for this was right: The only true reason for literature was

---

* More from *In Memoriam*.

the grandly moral, the grandly spiritual. And how to achieve this except by some belief?

I write the word *great*, but in what way great if no belief sustains the greatness? Suspend judgment, and, at least in the writing and in the reading too, give in to the great vision? Or believe outright? Write for love. Dare to allow the expression its eternal fullness, and eliminate all that limits such fullness in the daily. Eliminate the furniture, the plates and cups, the pictures, the socks drying on the radiator, and allow the space as an essential, the essential light-filled space, in which occurs:

So, word by word, and line by line,
The dead man touched me from the past,
And all at once it seemed at last
The living soul was flashed on mine . . .

I was invited by the secretary of the Chetwynd Society, Martin, to a garden party. The colors of the society's tie were white, black, and purple, obligatory for male and female members. Martin hoped for much polite and earnest conversation, and promised the occasion to be most enjoyable.

The Menu

* * *

Pâté, French Bread, Butter

* * *

York Ham on the Bone

Cold Chicken

Salads

* * *

Strawberries, Cream

* * *

Cheese

* * *

Fresh Fruit

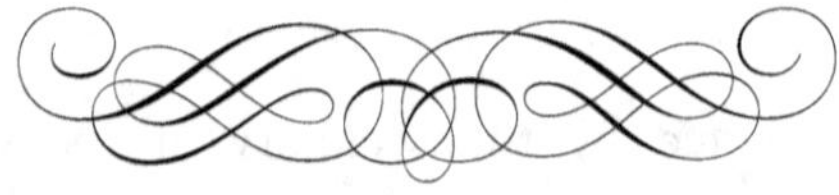

Jean Pericot Methode Champanoise was to flow freely, at the cost of £0.75 per guest, a check to that amount, made out to the secretary, to be left in his pigeonhole as soon as possible.

Martin flitted from person to person, wanting to get everyone drunk on the cheap Spanish champagne—not really champagne—and worried because rain began to fall. Umbrellas were opened and some went for shelter in the entrances of the Bodleain Library stairways. The food, on long tables, was covered with white plastic tarpaulin in which water collected. Whenever the rain stopped, the closed umbrellas were stuck upside down in the lawn, and everyone came out from the entrances, and everyone drank, and when it rained again, everyone remained in the rain, wet. There were piggyback races, the undergraduate females carrying, staggering, the males, and falling onto the sodden grass. Bottles of the cheap bubbly were in a cardboard carton on the riverbank, and bottle after bottle was taken from the carton and opened so the corks would pop out into the river, aimed, if possible, at slowly passing punts. Martin went about groping "all the straight men—well, most of them were straight, some so-so." A group of men gathered round Martin and lifted him, screaming, and, one-two-three, swung him back and forth.

I said to an undergraduate, "I hope he can fly."

And he said, "Of course he can fly. He's a fairy."

Martin was thrown into the Cam.

One chorister attending said he had invitations to seven garden parties in one day for May week.

I saw the undergraduates emerging from their exams in tee shirts, shorts, and sandals, into the warm, sunlit air.

Having sat for their Tripos, they would go wild.

Three male undergraduates came to my rooms at night, about eleven o'clock, drunk. They'd been drinking since they'd finished their exams the past afternoon. Laughing, joking, they sprawled on my sofa and chairs.

As free as they would ever be in their lives, some of those who had come to my sessions returned to, they said, tempt me out to walk with them along the Cam, and about blossoming cherry trees and red tulips, bluebells, forget-me-nots, dandelions, all in high grass. And in the King's Fellows' Garden, I, feeling as free as they did for a while, sat with them on the grass, then there was the walk through the back gate of King's, on either side wild cow parsley, and stopping on the bridge to look at punters on the Cam. In what way do I remember one punt filled with young people, boys and girls, who fell over and over into the heavy green water; pulled back into the punt, their clothes, and especially their white shirts or blouses, clinging to them? Beyond them was King's Chapel.

I would leave in a few weeks. In my rooms, I looked out of my open window at Webb's Court, filled, too, with warm, sunlit air. In the parterre, the budlia—I think it was budlia—was in full bloom. Someone from the pantry or buttery was wheeling a tea tray across the court; the dishes and cups rattled.

Day after day of totally clear sunlight.

Sometimes alone, sometimes with others, I walked in the English countryside, where the English ideals asserted themselves in densities of laburnum, lilac, broom; ideals kept unpretentious (nothing pretentiously cared for, natural, or seemingly so) by tangles of honeysuckle. And a walk through a little woods, the floor covered in bluebells, and out of the woods, along a path along the edge of a field high with cow parsley, in the distance a copse of chestnut trees in blossom, white and pink, and beyond the chestnut trees, on a low rise, the bright yellow of rape, and beyond that the clear pale blue English sky.

About the Author

David Plante grew up in Providence, Rhode Island, within a French-Canadian parish that was palisaded by its language, a French that dated from the time of the first French colonists in the early seventeenth century to what was then most of North America, la Nouvelle France. Plante has been inspired to write novels rooted in La Nouvelle France, most notably in *The Family*, a contender for the National Book Award. His renowned book, *Difficult Women*, a nonfiction work that profiled Jean Rhys, Sonia Orwell, and Germaine Greer, was reissued by *The New York Review of Books Press* in 2017. His most recent book, *Eternity*, was published by Green City Books in 2024. He has dual nationality, American and British, but lives in Lucca, Italy.

www.ingramcontent.com/pod-product-compliance
Lightning Source LLC
LaVergne TN
LVHW010840120826
845149LV00017B/3322

* 9 7 8 1 9 6 3 1 0 1 1 2 6 *